NIGHT OF THE STALKERS

BY JASON RIDER

Bellissima Publishing, LLC
Jamul, California
www.bellissimapublishing.com

This book is fictional. Any resemblance to actual persons living or dead or to any events, current or past, is purely coincidental.

Copyright © 2007 by Jason Giacchino, aka Jason Rider

All rights reserved. No part of this book may be reproduced or transmitted in any means, whether mechanical, electronic, photocopying or recording, or any by or through any information storage and retrieval system without express written permission from the publisher and author.

Published by Bellissima Publishing, LLC, Jamul, California
www.bellissimapublishing.com

Printed in the United States of America

ISBN 0-9793358-2-5
First Edition

'For my parents for their continued support'

*'For Raymond Jordano and his sharing of the
Light that will not dim'*

NIGHT OF THE STALKERS

BY JASON RIDER

Night Of The Stalkers

PROLOGUE

Tucker O'Doyle awoke gasping for air. He caught his breath and looked around at the familiar gray stone walls of his bedroom high within the stone castle, Losparia. Judging by the light that spilled into his small oval window it was already late morning.

"Petri," he called softly.

A plump green bird with a long crooked beak sprang to life, suddenly awakened by Tucker's voice.

"Yes sir," the bird responded from its perch above Tucker's massive bed.

"Fetch my wand please."

Tucker slid out of bed. He felt the cold hard stone with the bottoms of his bare feet. He let out a long deep yawn as Petri dropped the wand from his beak into Tucker's lap.

"The dream again your majesty," Petri asked as he returned to his perch with a trail of green tail feathers dancing to the ground behind him.

"Yes, it's Mister Harvey, Petri. I think he's in trouble. I keep having this awful dream of him falling away from me. How long has it been since I last saw him?"

The bird cocked its head, and then slowly blinked.

"I believe it has been two of your years, sire."

Tucker frowned. It hadn't seemed like so long. He waved his wand above a mug of dried herbs sending steaming hot water from the wand's tip into the cup of herbs magically changing it into broth. With a flick of his wrists, he sent his slippers sliding across the stone floor and onto his awaiting feet.

"I'm going to have to go back, Petri. I have to talk to him."

"The senate would never let you leave, your majesty. Why don't you send your advisors to the other side to greet him?"

"I've tried," Tucker sighed with a sip of his morning tea. "They make excuses. They stall by bogging me down with bureaucracy and proceedings."

The bird cocked its head. It scratched its folded wings with its beak.

"There's something wrong, Petri. I feel it when I sleep and although I cannot yet practice spells of the Green Crystal, I fear it is the future that concerns me."

"You would be wise to not fret about such things your highness. Today you meet with General Garrut. You mustn't keep him waiting again."

"I know." Tucker said as he finished his tea. He stood a moment longer, starring blankly at the wall before approaching his clothing chest.

CHAPTER ONE

The Senate

Dressed in honorary purple robes, Tucker took his seat at the Throne of Nespa' as the senate members gathered. He came to know many of the hundred members quite well individually during his two years as king. He was particularly fond of Shreif, the village leader and representative of the Forest Farrows. He built a close friendship with Ogle, one of the many Zoobles he had helped set free. Today the party gathered and marched quietly march to their seats around the throne room. There had been a lot of argumentative meetings between the representatives lately. Tucker was growing tired of the endless debates. Part of the trouble stemmed from Witi-Quay, the Slosh Worm representative from the shores of Sand Crest. He looked exactly like the horrible segmented white worm that tried to take Tucker's life on the beach. Witi-Quay was more civilized, but he shared many of his kindred's savage viewpoints. He fought for legislation to legalize creature-trading whenever the topic was brought to the floor. Tucker did his best to remind himself that Witi-Quay had nothing to do with the trader who had captured Vanle. Some days that was easier to do than others.

The massive General Garrut entered the throne room last. He was forced to crouch into the main entrance of the chamber to fit through it. Its furry body throbbed with hints of solid muscle below its coat of black matted fur. Razor sharp talons clicked on the stone floor as it approached the table. The room fell silent. The massive Night Stalker folded its leathery wings up against its back and glared at Tucker with cold marble-like eyes. Tucker fought off the chills. He tried not to look directly at the giant bat-like face.

"We have summoned representatives of the civilizations of Zooblatia here today to address concerns of security," a voice boomed from the center of the meeting table. "King Tucker O'Doyle, we begin at your command."

Tucker nodded, as he always did. The meetings were typically mediated by Hithrey, a neutral Sea Dweller like Oso with a surprisingly powerful voice.

"Very well, General Garrut, you have the floor."

The massive Night Stalker remained hunched over at the far end of the table opposite Tucker. It was unusually large and miserable even for one of its species, all of whom were larger than fully-grown men. It drew a deep breath. It showed no sign of emotion on its pink fleshy face.

"My forces report that constant three year patrols reveal no outside threats to the Zooblatian Mainland," he snarled. "I request an immediate mandate to downgrade our responsibilities."

The room exploded with bickering voices.

"Silence!" Hithrey shouted over the commotion. "We will come to order! Continue, General."

"My forces wish to return to their homeland of Nocoule under my discretion. We agreed to your king's legislation to colonize our homeland, but what good is your law if we are not there to enforce it?"

The members of the assembly turned to look at Tucker to see his reaction. Voices mumbled across the massive chamber.

"King Tucker O'Doyle, your ruling on this matter, please." Hithrey said.

Tucker felt the Night Stalker's cold penetrating eyes bore into him. He swallowed hard. He tried not to lock gazes with the massive creature.

"Very well," Tucker said after an uncomfortable moment of deliberation. "Tell your troops to return to their home land when they are no longer needed here."

The crowd erupted in protest.

"But your majesty" a representative seated to Tucker's left interrupted.

"Our people are defenseless without a central army," another interjected.

"Order," Hithrey called out again. "The king has made his decision."

General Garrut bowed his head with a look of disgust rather than respect. Then he turned away from the meeting and ducked through the main entrance way. Tucker sensed from the beginning the Night Stalkers were not tolerant of the senate's procedures and cared even less for taking orders from a boy.

"Does any of the representatives want to discuss another matter at this council meeting?"

Voices filled the room. They came from all directions of the meeting table. Hithrey slammed the Carock down onto the stone table's surface. It sent blue sparks and smoke into the air. The room was silent.

"Does anyone have any matter to discuss that does not pertain to today's ruling?"

The room remained silent.

"Then this meeting is concluded. Members objecting to the ruling may begin the appeals process. Meanwhile, the king's order stands."

Tucker nodded.

Night Of The Stalkers

"The meeting is dismissed."

Everyone left the room squawking and squabbling, and fighting amongst themselves as they made their exits.

CHAPTER TWO

The Escape Plan

Tucker hurried up to his room. He skipped up the winding stone steps of the rear corridor. Although the meeting concluded, the conference chambers rarely emptied immediately. In fact, Tucker was certain such a controversial ruling would spark hours of continued debating and a lengthy appeals process that could drag on until half of the senate members voted to overrule Tucker's decision. His old life was a lonely one, but it *wasn't* political. Sometimes he couldn't help wondering if having no opinion was better than having to make so many decisions.

Tucker swung his door open. Then he quickly closed it, and he locked it behind him. Petri jumped to attention. Clearly, he was sleeping again.

"How was the meeting your majesty?"

Tucker grinned.

"I'm glad it's over with old friend," he said as he removed the ceremonial robes. "Say Petri, I can trust you to perform a task for me right?"

"Oh no, not this again," the bird cried out in objection.

"Yes Petri," Tucker said as a stream of sparkling dust fell from his wand. "Just make certain you don't unlock this door for anyone until I return."

"But your highness, you have Silver Crystal training with Princess Vanle this afternoon."

"I'll be back long before then," Tucker said as he looked over his shoulder, "besides you worry too much."

"I am responsible for you sir."

"Nobody's going to know, Petri. I have to get out of this stuffy castle every now and then."

Tucker pulled back the crimson sash that covered his window.

"A morning this beautiful shouldn't be wasted indoors anyway."

"Do hurry back sire and be careful."

Tucker climbed onto the ledge of his small oval window and in a flash pushed himself into free-fall. The ground rushed up to greet him but not before his wand blasted to sparkling white life, pulling a gust of rising wind up to slow his descent. He continued to draw the wind harder and faster until his feet touched softly upon

Night Of The Stalkers

the fluffy green grass outside the courtyard. A glance over his left shoulder ensured none of the castle guards had spotted him. It was a pretty good dash to reach the cover of the forest and a great morning for a run. Tucker drew a deep breath of fresh morning air and made haste to escape toward the river.

Several hours of quiet reflection slipped past. Tucker sat beside the river watching its deep blue whirling currents turn white as they crashed along the rocks. Tucker watched as Zooblatia's twin suns danced together across the late morning sky, casting hues of pink through the white flowered trees. Since the fall of the Darkor nearly three years earlier, the entire land seemed enveloped in serenity. Tucker liked to roam the countryside when he felt daring enough to break free of the invisible bounds that came with being king. Perhaps it was because he was forced to sneak on borrowed time that he came to appreciate silent moments. Why he chose to hide away in his parents' basement in his old life was a complete mystery to him. The joys of being outdoors o0nly became apparent to him after his induction ceremony. The cold hard castle walls caused him to crave for wide-open spaces, warm breezes, and fresh air.

Tucker tiptoed quietly across the grass fields, returned to the courtyard's edge and took out his wand. He mumbled to himself then whirled the sparkling white wand upward. With a hard leap, he caught the gusting updraft that rose beneath him and rode the current up the castle wall. He caught the window recess with his free hand, rolled into the opening and landed softly in his bed. Petri leapt from his perch in response and flopped to the floor; his wings spread in fear.

"Must you enter so abruptly your highness?"

Tucker dusted himself off with a smile.

"I thought you're ready for anything."

"While you were out gallivanting sire, the princess has been waiting for you in the western corridor. I suggest you hurry. She and Castle Keep Krump are getting awfully suspicious."

"I'm on my way," Tucker said, and he dashed off toward the western wing of the castle. "Thanks for the help Petri."

Vanle looked mildly unimpressed as Tucker burst into the training room out of breath. His clothing was disheveled. His hair was a mess.

"Prompt as always," Castle Keep Krump said with her usual sarcastic tone.

"I'm sorry had to wait, Vanle," Tucker said as he nervously tapped his wand into his left palm.

"It's no bother," the tiny Forest Farrow said as she revealed a silver wand of her own. "Have you been practicing your Silver Crystal Techniques?"

"I will leave you two to your lessons," Krump said as she picked up the tiny teacup from which Vanle had been drinking.

13

Night Of The Stalkers

The moment she exited the room Tucker took a seat. He ran his fingers through his hair. Krump had to have been as old as the castle itself. She was a stiff gray furred old goat that stood upright on wobbly legs. Her main purpose was to keep the castle tidy. Somehow she became Tucker's unrequited nanny. He was convinced he could manage without her help, but her help came nonetheless. Perhaps Tucker wouldn't have minded her guidance if she wasn't always so cranky.

"What have you learned to channel since our last lesson?" Vanle asked.

"I've gathered several sparrows, and I caused fish to jump out of the water as I stood at the edge of the river."

"No Adacore?" Vanle asked, disappointed in Tucker's lack of progress.

"No. I have not been able to draw in a wild Adacore. I don't understand why. Perhaps it's because they are too big and too unpredictable."

"Why King O'Doyle, I am forced to pretend I did not just hear you say they're too big. Size has nothing to do with the power of the crystals. I have used this very wand, a toothpick to *your* eyes, to channel beasts from the deep sea that are *larger* than this castle."

Tucker kneeled and brought himself down to Vanle's eye level and told her with a smile, "I know. That is why you are the teacher, and I am the student."

The tiny Farrow shook her head with a grin.

"Come on," she said as she climbed onto Tucker's hand, "let's go outside where we can get some work done."

The courtyard was washed in bright midday heat. Vanle had been effortlessly demonstrating her abilities by attracting a long secession of sparrows that danced and twirled in perfect relationship with the movements of her tiny wand.

"I'm going to pass control over to you now," she said as she kept her attention on the birds.

Tucker raised his wand and briefly closed his eyes to clear his mind.

"Remember," Vanle added, "focus all of the Silver Crystal energy into your wand."

Tucker took a deep breath. He allowed himself the mental clarity to sort through the swirling invisible rings of energy that surrounded them. He had become adept at separating the various energy forces into appropriate crystal categories. The Silver Crystal force was more elusive to him than the White Crystal force that seemed to be everywhere. Silver Crystal energy was more fragile and delicate and, like the Forest Farrows themselves, surprisingly powerful. Tucker located the Silver Crystal energy force in his mind. Then he focused its effect onto his wand. The wand became alive with sparkling silver in direct response. He raised his wand toward the line of birds.

Night Of The Stalkers

"I feel you now," Vanle said as she lowered her wand. "Slow and steady," she directed.

The presence of the birds felt like wind against his wand. Each movement of his hand, however subtle, moved the line as he moved. He continued controlling their flight for a few moments before Vanle asked him to break the spell.

"Let's see how you handle the release," she said.

Tucker closed his eyes again. This time he allowed the Silver Crystal energy to dissipate from his wand. Instantly, the shimmering wand faded to black. The birds broke their formation and flew off in different directions.

"Very good, Tucker," Vanle said approvingly. "You practiced your technique."

"Daily," Tucker said, lost in a daydream.

"What's wrong?"

Tucker gathered his thoughts and looked down at the Forest Farrow who stood only a little higher than his ankle.

"Vanle, I'm having terrible dreams about Mister Harvey. I fear he's in trouble."

Vanle frowned.

"It's been so long since I've seen him or my parents. I think I would feel better if I knew everything back home was all right."

"I wish there was something I could do," Vanle said.

"There is," Tucker told her. "When you return to the Hidden Village tonight, you can deliver a message for me."

"To whom?"

"I need you to send Treol to the castle."

"Is that all?" Vanle asked.

"Tell him to keep the voyage secret. There are many senate spies who like to keep track of such things."

"I'll consider it an order from the king, your majesty."

Tucker smiled warmly at his tiny companion.

"You've been a true friend to me Princess Vanle. I don't know what I would do without you."

"Don't thank me now," she said as she climbed into the saddle of her awaiting Grass Rat. "I haven't delivered your message *yet*."

"Well, I thank you anyway," Tucker said as he waved goodbye to his friend. "Consider it gratitude in advance."

"Let us hope my early return to the Hidden Village draws no suspicion," she replied.

CHAPTER THREE

The Arrival

Several quiet weeks had passed since the day of General Garrut's meeting. The army slowly established a schedule of transit to and from their mysterious volcanic island home. Each morning Tucker watched from his bedroom as flocks of the giant bats flew in from the sea. At dusk the process repeated itself with divisions of troops departing from the Zooblatian mainland. The senate members were mysteriously quiet about the whole affair, far too quiet. The Night Stalkers performed their usual patrols on time and in good formation. The borders were safe and secure. Perhaps everyone was overreacting to Tucker's initial decision. After all, who could sympathize more with the concept of missing home than Tucker?

Night Of The Stalkers

A knock on Tucker's heavy bedroom door brought him back into focus.

"Tucker," a voice said from behind the wooden door, "there is a guest here to see you."

"Please send the guest in, Castle Keep Krump."

The door slowly opened. A tiny guest in a green cloak and matching hat appeared.

"Treol!" Tucker shouted, as he rushed over to greet his old friend.

"I would have arrived sooner," the Forest Farrow said while he slipped off his hat in respect, "but it was my rotation for village night watch."

"Oh it's no problem my friend, no problem at all. I'm just happy your journey was safe."

"I took unmapped routes and traveled by dark sky," Treol whispered. "The princess told me to keep my voyage secret."

"I *knew* I could count on you. I need a travel companion. Can you spare a few days?"

The tiny Forest Farrow smiled.

"Of course, Tucker. I can spare as long as you need."

"The voyage must be kept secret. There are many spies in these lands who would report my absence to the senate."

"You mean they don't already know you are leaving?"

Tucker shook his head.

Night Of The Stalkers

"I cannot let them know, Treol. They would ask me to send aides in my place. I need to take this trip myself."

"If you don't mind me asking, where are we going?"

"We're going back toward Appelia, into the river caves and through the portal that led me here. I need to see Mr. Harvey. I have a *terrible* feeling something is *wrong*."

Treol looked up at his friend with a nod of approval.

"I will be by your side no matter how long it takes."

Tucker rose early the next morning, before the first sunrise. Petri slept noisily on his bedside perch. He snored continuously. Treol was still sleeping on top of Tucker's clothing chest, wrapped in scarves that draped down onto the stone floor. Tucker went over his plan in his head a final time. He had given the plan *months* of consideration. He was certain he had everything covered. His plan was based on the premise there would be a three day break between senate meetings. Without the worry of bureaucracy, his only difficulty would be escaping Castle Keep Krump. She was terribly meddlesome of late, insisting on frequent room inspections among other annoyances. Tucker was awake half the night attempting to learn a Silver Crystal spell from Treol, a spell, if executed properly, which might be the right tool to keep the old goat out of his affairs.

He gently shook Treol. His friend woke up and was alert and ready.

"Okay Treol," Tucker whispered, "here we go."

Tucker raised his wand. Treol muttered a few quiet words. The wand shimmered with silver light so bright it illuminated the entire room. The wand wiggled in Tucker's hand. He fought its energy until Treol finished the spell. With a blast of release and an immediate cooling of the wand in Tucker's hand, a beam of silver smoke shot forth into Petri who continued to snore loudly.

"Did it work?" Tucker asked.

He returned the wand into the belt of his robes.

"There's only way to be sure," Treol responded.

Tucker approached Petri and gently patted the top of his green feathered head. The bird's eyes slowly opened.

"Come back later!" Petri cried out. "I'm not feeling too well."

"Wow," Tucker said, unable to hide his excitement. "It sounds just like me!"

"It should last a few days," Treol said as he rolled up the scarf, "after which Petri will return to normal with no memory of the time he was under the spell."

"Then we have no time to lose."

"I'm busy practicing my crystal spells," Petri called out again in Tucker's voice.

"Do you have everything, Treol?" Tucker asked as he slid free his window sash.

Night Of The Stalkers

The Forest Farrow nodded and slipped his quiver of arrows over his shoulder.

"Climb into my hand. I've mastered a White Crystal spell that'll get us down to the courtyard safely."

"Come back later," Petri blurted out in Tucker's voice. "I'm not feeling too well."

Tucker barely touched the ground before he dashed off into the cover of the nearby pines. He slipped across the dry forest floor without looking over his shoulder. He crossed through a tangled thicket. Then he sprinted into an open field. Out of breath, he knelt down to the ground and set Treol on the tall grass.

"It looks like we made it my friend," he said as he squinted in the dual afternoon sunlight. "Now we need to summon something fast enough to get us down to Appelia"

"An Adacore would get us there by early dusk," Treol responded.

"I haven't the skill to summon one yet."

Treol looked at his companion with surprise.

"I should be able to get us one with a well placed arrow," he said; "but you'll have to use your wand to calm and control it."

Tucker agreed even though he doubted his ability to do as his friend suggested.

Treol drew an arrow from his quiver and shook a stream of silver glitter from its tip that vanished before hitting the ground.

"The trick is going to be finding one at this hour," he said as he practiced his aim. "It could be some time."

Tucker drew his wand and cleared his thoughts. He felt distracted by thoughts of the senate and their spies, and thoughts of Castle Keep Krump ignoring Petri's words and entering his chambers. He felt a constant chaos of doubt about everything. The feeling of calmness grew stronger with each of his crystal lessons, but he still felt its presence in him. There was an unseen harmony between the castle walls, the stone floors, and the open spaces beyond. Tucker learned to enter a place in his mind and to focus it into his wand. He closed his eyes, and he allowed the warmth of the suns to envelop him. He felt the life all around. Treol's stout heart appeared as a ball of silver light in his mind. Worms silently passed beneath their feet, and tiny birds bobbed up and down in the branches of the trees. He reached out beyond the immediate vicinity and searched with his mind for the unique presence of an Adacore. His mind wandered across the fields and high above the tops of the trees. He envisioned the rock formations of the plains beyond and flew through the endless clouds that rolled over the sea. Then, without warning, he found one. It was a thought really, a shapeless vision as unmistakable as if he had seen it with his own eyes. It was an Adacore in drifting flight high above the sea. His wand shimmered into silver life.

"You found one?" Treol asked in amazement.

Night Of The Stalkers

Tucker called to it and asked it to seek him out in the center of the grassy field. The connection was unmistakable. Then Tucker returned to reality. The vision was lost to the suns' bleached field around them.

"I called it, Treol!" he exclaimed. "It heard my thoughts!"

Treol scanned the horizon, and he pulled his tiny green derby down to shade his eyes.

"Look!" he exclaimed as he pointed westward. "Here it comes!"

A tiny spec on the distant horizon steadily grew in size until its unique shape became clear. A massive Adacore sailed closer with wings wide in flight. It passed before the lower sun, shortly disappearing from sight, and then it reappeared to Tucker's squinting eyes. Treol lowered his bow.

"Treol you'll need to fire that arrow," Tucker said.

"No, you've got him," Treol replied with a smile. "It is because of your command he seeks us."

Tucker noticed his wand shimmered and sparkled as the giant winged beast grew closer. Its massive talon claws touched softly on the grass before them, its wings folded tightly against its back. The Adacore cocked its head to look at Tucker and Treol with its right eye. Tucker could hear it, not as a voice or thought but as a feeling. It was waiting for his command and answering him through the wand. Tucker didn't need to say anything. He didn't even have to think of the route in his mind. He and Treol quickly mounted the Adacore's awaiting flank and situated themselves behind the creature's feathered neck. With a wave of the wand they were off, holding onto the creature any way they could as it hopped and leapt. It flapped its wings and the ground spiraled away beneath them. Tucker took a deep breath. The heart pounding dizziness of flight kept him from savoring the excitement of the reality he was controlling an Adacore on his own.

CHAPTER FOUR

Touching Down

The suns shined brightly as they silently passed high above the Zooble village of Appelia. Tucker fought back his desire to detour there. It had been several years since he last saw his friend Curious and the village. From their vantage point he could see the spinning water wheel and belt driven sprinklers watering the crops. He felt happiness and contentment through the wand. It was like a warm white cloud washing over him from far below.

The outline of the river snaked through the hillside like a blue pencil line. The caves came into view. Almost instinctively the Adacore began to slowly descend, its wings locked spread wide. The river looked exactly like he had remembered it. Its water rushed noisily between its rocky banks. Wisps of white water smacked around protruding rocks and turned gray in deeper pools.

Night Of The Stalkers

The Adacore landed on the bank at the water's edge. Then it lowered itself to a kneel to allow a dismount. The cave entrance was dark and wide, a mouth that endlessly swallowed the river's waters. Tucker instructed the Adacore to wait until they returned. He focused his wand until he felt a bubble of cool air surround him. Treol perched on his shoulder. He stepped cautiously into the quickly moving water. The White Crystal spell kept him dry and clean as he stumbled across the jagged riverbed.

"We made good time," he said. "Perhaps I'll have enough time to visit my parents."

They passed into the darkness of the cavern. Tucker held the wand at arm's length, allowing its white shimmer to cast its shadowy light about the cave. They ventured deeper inside, following the gradually shifting walls of rock until the light of day appeared in the distance.

"That's funny," Tucker said. "I don't recall going this deeply into the cave."

The light of day grew steadily larger until they reached the cave's exit, a massive opening in which the river's water tumbled wildly into the far below sea. Tucker peered over the giant waterfall, and then quickly spun around. In the other direction, his eyes focused through the cave's darkness towards a tiny ball of light from the side where they entered.

Night Of The Stalkers

"This can't be!" Tucker cried out in despair. "The portal is gone!"

"Are you sure we're in the right cave?"

"Yes I'm sure," Tucker said with his fingers pointed forward. "It was there in the middle of the cave."

"I don't understand what could have happened," Treol said.

"It was here, I'm telling you, at this exact spot! There were beams of purple and pink light swirling around each other."

They walked slowly back through the cave. The middle appeared no different than the rest of the cavern. All they found was rocky walls, spiky ceilings, and a floor of white rapids. Treol just stood there, momentarily dumbfounded. Then he walked the entire length of the cave a dozen times.

As they sat on the bank next to the Adacore, Tucker fought the burning tears welling in his eyes.

"I'm trapped here," he said. "I can't get back home."

Treol scampered along the shore in silent observation. The second sun was setting. It cast an eerily gray shadow. Treol squinted. Then he called out above the roar of the river:

"There are creatures near the river's bend. We would be wise to take flight."

Tucker immediately gained his composure. They mounted the patiently awaiting Adacore. They looped around the shore and passed safely above the cavern's roof, out over the open sea.

Night Of The Stalkers

"Have you planned our next destination?" Treol asked.

"I haven't little buddy" Tucker said. He shook his dizzy head. "I just don't know."

Several silent hours passed. Only the wind rustled through Tucker's hair. The Adacore floated gracefully through the misty clouds above the calm of the sea until the last light of dusk was lost beyond the horizon. Tucker was mentally exhausted from the circle of thoughts and fears that revolved endlessly through his mind. His recent dreams of Mr. Harvey filled him with a deep sensation of dread that now coupled with his sadness that he could not make contact with his parents. Zooblatia had become a lonely place, a prison without walls. As Treol slept peacefully in the folds of Tucker's robe, he fought back the confusion that consumed him. Then he decided to return to the castle to rest. Perhaps there would be another opportunity to seek home, if a logical plan developed in the light of day. As he thought about it, the Adacore responded, and banked sharply back toward the shoreline. Tucker debated using his White Crystal spell to stir wind to their backs, but found he could not bring forth the energy. He sat forward and gazed at the empty vastness before him. This was *his* kingdom.

They arrived at the courtyard just before dawn. The misty fields that lead up to the stone gates were cold and slippery. The Adacore had been nervous since they cleared the pines. It was impossible to tell by looking at it, but Tucker felt the disturbance through the wand. The feeling was magnified by an eerie silence surrounding the massive stone castle. Treol continued sleeping as Tucker carefully approached the area below his chamber window.

"You are free to go," he whispered to the great Adacore as they landed and he got off the great bird with Treol still asleep in his pocket.

The giant animal cocked its head in confirmation, but it did not take flight. Tucker shrugged and looked at the Adacore.

"Suit yourself," he said.

He took out his wand with its soft white shimmer and began to stir the air beneath him. He paused a moment before unleashing the gust of wind that would send him skyward. There was something out of place. A surge of fear welled up inside him. He dismissed it because of either his lack of sleep or his discovery the portal had disappeared. He took another look around him. The Adacore still sat patiently near the forest's edge. With another wave of his wand, Tucker rose with the wind toward his open window and slipped quietly inside. The Adacore watched apprehensively.

CHAPTER FIVE

Trap Sprung

The wand lit Tucker's room and allowed him to find his way in the dark.

"Treol!" Tucker cried out loudly, as he looked around his room. "Something is terribly wrong!"

The tiny Forest Farrow sprang to consciousness. He flipped free of Tucker's robe. He drew an arrow before his feet hit the stone floor. Tucker concentrated his energy to increase the wand's intensity. It glowed brightly, showering the room with soft white light. The door had been destroyed, splintered as if struck with a battle axe. The room was charred, the tapestries burnt, the books scattered, and the bed was a mess of feathers and shredded fabric. Treol put his ear to the floor.

"There appears to be no one on this level or the level below," he whispered.

Tucker squinted. He attempted to make sense of the situation. They heard a scratching sound coming from under the bed. Treol wheeled around. He pulled his bowstring. A small green shape hopped from beneath the pile of bed feathers.

"Come back later," it said in Tucker's voice. "Come back later."

"Petri," Tucker exclaimed, as he dropped to his knees. "I'm so glad you're all right."

Treol removed his arrow from the bow string and waved his left hand.

"The spell is lifted. Nevertheless, he cannot help us. He will remember nothing of the events that took place here."

"Your highness," the bird squawked in its usual tone. "Where am I?"

He looked around and moved erratically, like a miniature version of an Adacore.

"Your majesty, what happened?"

"I don't know Petri," Tucker said as he returned to his feet. "We're going to find out."

The green bird flew and perched on Tucker's left shoulder. Treol ran toward the shattered doorway.

"What do you see?" Tucker asked.

"There is no motion in the corridor and no sound in the stairwell."

"Stay close. We'll go down together."

Treol marched closely to the right of Tucker's stride. He aimed his bow to coincide with the movements of his head. The twisting stairwell was silent and dark. Even the wand's intense light was gobbled up by the heavy shadows all around. The lower stairwell door had been destroyed. It was ripped cleanly from its iron hinges and thrown aside. The gathering room was charred. The cinder smoke rose in slow curling lines through the wand's light. Treol jumped onto the oak table's splintered surface. He lowered his bow and scanned the room. Tucker entered.

"No activity here," he whispered, "at least not now."

"These coals are still hot," Tucker said, as he looked at what was once a wooden spice rack. "Whatever happened here must have happened recently."

"The castle fell under attack," Treol told Tucker. "These aren't normal burn marks. They're too concentrated. They aren't random like a natural fire."

"But who could have. . ."

"I don't know," Treol interrupted. "It would appear they've mastered a crystal's ability controlling flame."

Tucker felt his heart sink.

Night Of The Stalkers

"But I thought the Magenta Crystal was responsible for fire spells? We destroyed the Magenta Crystal."

"Yes," the Farrow responded. "However, fire can be mastered through the power of many elemental crystals. I have seen elders use the power of the White Crystal to make open flame. I fear this attack could have been the product of any one of a dozen elemental crystals."

"Then who did this?" Tucker asked as he remembered Castle Keep Krump must have been on the grounds during the attack.

"Follow me," he directed Treol.

They dashed down several corridors and crossed many more massive rooms that were damaged. Smoke lingered everywhere. Small pockets of burning fabric and wood littered the floors. Treol jumped about the debris with uncanny gracefulness as he kept up with Tucker's frantic flailing.

Castle Keep Krump's chamber doors were burned cleanly through. Her normally tidy little room was ravaged and empty. Tucker hung his head in defeat and leaned his sweaty palm against the smoldering doorframe.

"Tucker," Treol called out, "something approaches!"

Tucker turned to see the silhouette of something approaching them through the haze of the curing smoke clouds. It was tall and slender and drew shallow breaths of loud rasping air. Treol released an arrow that intentionally smashed into the wall just to the creature's right. The arrow exploded into a rain-shower of hot silver spark. It illuminated the approaching stranger. Tucker recognized its fowl appearance immediately. It was Witi-Quay, the white segmented worm of the senate. Only this time the creature didn't move right. Treol drew another arrow as the worm's face fell back into shadow. Tucker nodded toward his small companion. Before Treol could fire again, Witi-Quay tumbled forward, landing flat against the hard stone floor. The light of the wand spilled on the creature's body. It was charred and slashed. It attempted to lift its broad head, but its coal-black eyes rolled slowly back into its head before it could get its chin off the ground. With an uncontrollable wave that traveled down its rows of stubby legs, Witi-Quay died at Tucker's feet. Treol eased his bow and looked up at Tucker in surprise. Petri dug his talons into Tucker's shoulder.

"Who could have done this?" Tucker asked.

Treol continued to move down the shadowy corridor. The first light of dawn found its way into the stained glass cathedral of the main entrance room. Hues of purple and blue made a pattern of checkers across the massive open floor. For a moment the reality of the horror around them was lost to the serenity of morning. In a few hours Tucker would have joined Castle Keep Krump in the great room for morning tea, before beginning daily studies.

"Tucker look!" he called out. "It appears the main gates haven't been disturbed."

Night Of The Stalkers

The wrought iron gates that stood behind the massive drawbridge were intact. Most of the locked doors in the castle had been destroyed by what appeared to be a heavy ax, and yet the main point of entry stood unscathed.

"The attackers were *inside* the castle's walls," Treol explained, and this confirmed Tucker's suspicions.

There *were* secret entrances into the stronghold Tucker vaguely recalled being shown years earlier. There was a hatch on the roof that led into the Eastern looking tower, and an underground tunnel that led to the structure's flooded foundation. The attack was too massive, too well orchestrated, and too destructive to have occurred through a single file march down rotten old ladders. The basement entrance was feasible, but Tucker doubted that route as well.

Suddenly, Tucker heard a ringing in his ears followed by a surge of dizziness that nearly caused his legs to buckle at the knees.

"I felt it too," Treol said before Tucker explained the sensation. "It's the Red Crystal."

"The Red Crystal?" Tucker asked.

"Yes. We're not out of danger yet. We need to get out of here."

Tucker struggled with the main gates. They clanked heavily through iron chains. Treol continued to scan the surroundings.

"There," he cried out in alarm.

Night Of The Stalkers

Tucker followed Treol's line of vision to a sparkling red wand jammed tightly into an arched stone ceiling support. It had been folded in half. Although it was not completely severed, it spilled flashes of white light from its middle. Tucker grabbed Treol to his chest and waved up an air current that sent the threesome sailing toward the corridor opposite the main gate. The wand snapped in two. The room was engulfed in hot flame. The fire would have incinerated them, but they broke through the stained glass window that lined the long passageway. They tumbled into the courtyard pond. There was a second explosion that split the castle apart at the seams. Through the muffled still of the cold water that surrounded them, Tucker felt the blast ripple. Pieces of flaming heavy stone and mortar tumbled into the water, splashes of white bubbles trailed behind. Tucker unleashed a dome of air around them. They came to rest at the pond's muddy floor. Giant pieces of stone and brick came slapping down around them. The debris stirred up clouds of murky water as they settled onto the bottom.

"Treol what happened?"

"A wand containing crystal essence contains powerful energy, strength from the very crystal itself. Should a wand be destroyed, the raw crystal energy is released. I have heard about this phenomenon. It is said only a more powerful crystal can destroy a wand. I am certain the explosion was no accident."

"What crystal could destroy a Red Crystal wand?"

"I cannot say. The village elders speak of a legend in which clashing crystals were said to have destroyed entire mountains in the days of old. Such knowledge is unknown to me."

Through the cloudy water above, Tucker could see the smoldering ruins of his castle. Thick black smoke rose slowly against the pale morning sky. Petri looked nervously around.

The damage up close was worse than Tucker had imagined. A vast blackened crater was all that remained of the center of Castle Losparia. Jagged chunks of twisted stone pointed skyward like a miniature colorless city. The main wall still stood as did the drawbridge. Behind the ruin appeared the cracked and tattered walls of the conference rooms and sleeping quarters. Smoke and dust filled the morning air. Treol removed his derby and bowed his head in a moment of silent respect at Tucker's side.

"We will deliver justice for this," Tucker murmured under his breath.

The Adacore retreated in fear to the surrounding pines. He returned once everything settled.

"We must make haste," Tucker said as he mounted the creature. "There is one who can help understand what has taken place."

Treol slipped his green derby over his head and took a post in the golden rope of Tucker's robes. With a wave of his hand, Tucker sent the Adacore rocketing skyward.

CHAPTER SIX

To Neveria

Tucker fell into a deep sleep during the slow flight into the Swamps of Neveria. The Adacore followed Tucker's commands flawlessly as he broke into the dense canopy of overlapping vines and thicket. He awoke to the sound of splashing as the giant bird landed on the black waters of the swamp. The grassy island home of Manaloul the Wise was in clear view.

Tucker dismounted. The foul water reached his waist. The Adacore dipped its head deep into the water and came up with a long spotted eel hanging limply from its beak. Tucker felt the presence of the Green Crystal. It was as though he wandered into a stream of emotions. He fought the sensation and kept his focus on the task at hand.

"I'm not sure it's wise to be venturing though the swamp!" Petri cried out.

"Don't worry, Petri. I have friends here."

A series of gurgling bubbles rose from the water, stopping Tucker in his tracks. Treol's eyes widened. The water parted around the rising hooded head of Manaloul. His appearance was always a bit startling to Tucker. This time was no exception. Four glassy orb-like eyes of red blinked slowly before them. Dripping tangles of plant-life hung from Manaloul's long sloped head.

"Welcome my weary travelers," he said in a soothing voice that made his alien appearance instantly disappear.

"It's good to see you again my old fiend," Tucker said as he bowed his head.

"Arise, your majesty. I know that it is with ill tidings you have returned to Neveria."

"We have many questions, Manaloul."

"We will find answers all of them. However, first you must follow me inside for a hot meal and some rest. The arm of our enemy finds no strength to strike here."

Manaloul led them into a discreet tunnel buried within the twisted tall grass of the highland. Tucker crouched to navigate into the widening chamber that opened up into a large clearing of stone with a ceiling of dripping white roots. Across from the room's entrance was a hearth that glowed brightly with crackling fire. Suspended above the flames was a large iron pot that boiled noisily. The air was damp, but warm. Tucker took a seat with Treol. Manaloul fetched a brown ladle from a rack.

"Let us eat to remind us hope is *never* lost, even when there *appears* to be *little* hope."

Tucker was handed a wooden bowl of steaming stew. The broth was creamy white. It smelled like wet grass. Tiny snails and mushrooms rolled around in the bowl. Manaloul handed a tiny cup of the stew to Treol, and sat down, across from Tucker, with a loud moan.

"So the walls of Losparia stand no longer. . ."

Tucker nodded.

"Castle Losparia stood throughout the ages as a remnant of a distant time of peace. It represented freedom and unity in a land once divided."

Tucker sipped his stew. It tasted bitter at first, but it became wonderfully warm and flavorful once it was swallowed.

"I was there, Tucker O'Doyle. My people stood guard at the pillared gates of Losparia. Where can we seek contentment when our symbol of peace is destroyed?"

"I do not know, Manaloul."

"We will find it in you, young friend. My peace is preserved by the fact you are safe and well."

"But who could have. . ."

"You did not come to here to ask who committed these heinous acts, did you? You already have the answer."

"The Night Stalkers," Treol replied.

"You've come to ask why," Manaloul continued. "It is always a question of why once we establish who."

"Well then," Tucker stammered, "why?"

"The question of why is a difficult one. Intention is often clouded by emotion. Emotion is often the result of twisted truth. The *why* in this case, is offset by a single error. Do you recognize the victory in our favor?"

"No," Tucker said, as he scratched his head. "It is hard to imagine us as victors in this dark hour."

"Our victory is they failed to destroy *you*. This was an attempt to destroy democracy and an assassination attempt on you. Let them remain blind in their ignorance. They do *not* know you live."

"But they destroyed the senate."

"If you can, imagine the senate as a ball of clay. The sculptor sits before me."

"What can I possibly do now, Manaloul? I'm a king without a castle, a ruler presumed dead by his subjects."

Night Of The Stalkers

"Your hour of bravery has yet to pass young king. Be grateful that to many you are considered dead. It is because of this the threat to your life is past. The Night Stalkers unleashed a threat Zooblatia has not witnessed since before the days of our ancestors."

"They've clashed crystals," Treol added.

"They've managed to unbalance that which exists through balance. They've knotted that which should never knot. The repercussions to this power could destroy all of the nations of our world, even if we united them to stand as one against them."

"The Night Stalkers must be destroyed the same way we destroyed the Darkor," Tucker said as he returned to his feet.

Manaloul returned to his bowl of stew.

"The journey will be perilous beyond my best preparation and will require an army unlike any other the free lands of Zooblatia has ever known. Where one could amass such a force is even beyond the vision of the Green Crystal."

"I will fight along your side," Treol said without hesitation.

"I will accompany you, but I won't return alive," Manaloul said.

"Then you won't come," Tucker told him. "You are far too important to the people of Zooblatia for me to risk losing you in battle."

"If you fail there will no longer be a people of Zooblatia to value my continued existence. Long have I foreseen the arrival of this hour; the hour in which the final keeper of the Green Crystal would face his destiny."

"Then," Tucker said as he felt his heart begin to sink, "if you were to be destroyed. . ."

". . . the Green Crystal would fade and be forever black."

"I can't let you do this Manaloul. If you've foreseen it, how can you allow yourself to be destroyed?"

"It is because the future does not play out like a vision. The future is only the emotion of the choices we make in the present. The Green Crystal does not make the future. We make the future in the now, in our every single choice. All we can do with the knowledge the crystal shares with us is to try to understand why we make the choices we make. The more difficult question to answer is the question of why."

"I can do it without you," Tucker said. "I'm experienced in this type of quest."

"The Nocoule Islands are larger than the Zooblatian mainland. They are uncharted, a dreadful place of volcano and ash inhabited by creatures of unspeakable terror. The seas around the islands boil."

"We've got Adacore and. . ."

"The air hangs heavy with a smog that would prove fatal even to an Adacore after prolonged exposure," Manaloul added .

Tucker dropped his spoon into the empty wooden bowl on his lap.

"We need to assemble a strike force to gain access to their stronghold and an army to attack from all sides once we are inside the stronghold."

"This is my fault," Tucker said after a long pause. "I trusted them to defend the kingdom, and I used them as my own personal guards."

"Even the Green Crystal could not see through their ruse, my young king. Emotion is a powerful disguise. I believe there is more behind this plot than the Night Stalkers realize."

Tucker sat forward, jarred by a startling fact he had nearly forgotten.

"The portal to my world has closed, Manaloul," he blurted.

"I know," Manaloul answered calmly. "It was closed by someone passing into our world from yours."

Tucker and Treol looked at each other in awe.

"Who from my world could have known?"

"I do not know," Manaloul replied, "but they brought in the long ago banished essence of the Gold Crystal. I feel it all around us."

"Banished?"

"Yes. It was hidden in your world long ago. As long as it remained there, the portal between the two worlds remained open."

Night Of The Stalkers

Tucker hung his head in defeat.

"I am sorry, Manaloul. Sorry to have brought all of this upon you and the races of Zooblatia. I'm the one who placed trust in the Night Stalkers."

Manaloul stood. He picked up the empty bowls.

"No need to apologize, young friend. It is because of your strong will you were not destroyed with the senate. Take this day to rest. I will meditate on the Green Crystal for guidance."

Tucker spent a majority of the day in restful recovery. He drifted in and out of sleep in the cozy nook of Manaloul's underground retreat. Treol remained at his side, sharpening his arrow tips and enchanting their surfaces with Silver Crystal spells. Petri perched on the wooden bedpost, sleeping calmly as if it was just another lazy day in the castle.

Manaloul returned by dusk with an armful of freshly caught fish. He removed his hooded robes and began to prepare the meal.

"What have you discovered?" Tucker asked from the bed.

"Many questions about the Gold Crystal remain unanswered. These questions are beyond the scope of vision the Green Crystal provides. At the time of the controversial Gold Crystal, I endured a painful personal tragedy of which I will not speak. My memory of details surrounding the account has grown dim. I must travel to Sand Crest in effort to seek what tattered record remains of these things."

"I didn't know records were kept," Tucker said as he quickly sat up.

"Many ages ago there were members of an elite group who devoted their entire lives to the study and recording of the behavior of the crystals. They were known as the Order of the Crystalline. They successfully cataloged thousands of entries, and their findings made clear the specific strengths and weaknesses of individual crystals. Spells were devised using their work as a map. That map is *still* used today. Unfortunately, their studies branched into the effects of crystals working together. The Order discovered crystals working in conjunction with each other were more potent and more unstable than the effects of any single crystal working alone. Word traveled of the study. Over time the members of the Crystalline Order began to disappear. No one ever discovered what happened to them. Nearly all their original work was destroyed. What remained was salvaged, reproduced, and locked away."

"In Sand Crest?"

"Yes, the knowledge was locked away in the larger cities and villages. I fear the destruction of Losparia is tied to this mystery, because the castle housed the original drafts of the Order's findings. No greater resource of the crystal combinations existed than that of the library of Losparia. Now it is forever gone."

"I will accompany you to Sand Crest. . ."

Night Of The Stalkers

"No," Manaloul insisted. "I must make this trek alone. Sand Crest is too public. I fear the taverns and pubs will crawl with assassins and enemy spies. It is best to offer no proof they failed to destroy you. Besides, I have a task for you to fulfill in my absence. Part of what you wonder can be answered better by those who were there."

Manaloul finished chopping the pink meat of the skinned and cleaned fish and slid it into a simmering pot above the hearth.

"Here," he said.

Manaloul took a small dried leaf from his table drawer and said, "Take this."

"What is it?" Tucker asked, as he opened his sweaty palm.

"This is the Leaf of Autuine. It is to be crushed and planted into the soil of Deadwood Pass."

"I don't understand. . ."

"Clear your mind of questions, young king. We will eat a hot meal and then part ways under the cover of darkness."

Treol packed his quiver with arrows and slid it over his shoulder. He flipped the bow neatly into place. It rested diagonally beneath the quiver. He put his derby on his head. Tucker got out of bed and nodded at his tiny companion.

"You stay here Petri," Tucker said.

"Gladly, your highness, I was thinking the same thing."

Night Of The Stalkers

"I shall return by dawn of the second day," Manaloul said. "Be extra cautious of those who might be spies and traitors. Leave no proof of your existence. I sense your mind is filled with question. Find hope, young friend, that in time all questions will be answered. Now, let us enjoy a brief meal before parting ways."

CHAPTER SEVEN

Deadwood Pass

Evening fell quickly in the eerie, mist-covered swamps. Tucker found it oddly discomforting to watch a hooded Manaloul vanish into the fog away from the serenity of his underground hut. He took the bridge to Sand Crest, while the path to Deadwood pass lead Tucker and Treol through the wetlands in the opposite direction. It was a very short flight by wing of the Adacore, but Manaloul insisted they travel by foot. Worse yet, Manaloul made them promise to keep their use of crystal spells to a minimum. Tucker found he now relied upon Treol's keen senses. Treol sat quietly at his post in the pocket of a tunic Tucker borrowed from Manaloul. The murky waters were too deep for someone of Treol's stature to navigate, and Tucker found it comforting to have an armed companion close and ready to defend. Besides, Manaloul made it clear Tucker needed to keep his face hidden with a hood in case enemy spies spotted him in transit.

Night Of The Stalkers

Despite his best efforts to be quiet, Tucker's footsteps splashed noisily through the marsh. The night air was surprisingly chilling; a cold Tucker felt in his exposed finger tips. The water that thoroughly soaked his feet felt warm as he slogged forward. Even with the faint glow of the wand to guide them, the blackness of night was thick and heavy. Tucker fought back his growing fear. He focused on the memory of Sand Crest and its busy populous. He silently wished he and Manaloul had traded tasks.

While no actual path existed through the marsh, Tucker found navigating to be a fairly straightforward process. Manaloul instructed Tucker to follow the open water straight through, promising that it would not pass waist-level. On the sides of the flooded opening there was thick patches of vegetation; twisted vines and low hanging branches. Tucker wore a sack of provisions Manaloul prepared prior to departure, salted meats, sweetened root, and skins of drinkable water.

"Something stirs to the west," Treol said as Tucker stopped in his tracks.

Tucker raised the wand slowly in an effort to cast more light into the thicket.

"Are you certain, Treol?"

The tiny Farrow readied his bow and arrow.

"I am certain. However, disturbing the unnamed occupants of the marsh may *not* be in our best interests."

Night Of The Stalkers

"We need to get out of here," Tucker whispered. "I need to channel the wind to our backs."

"Then all the magical beings for miles will recognize our presence. We should keep moving onward under the veil of darkness."

"You're right," Tucker said, as he resumed his march. "This path is perilous. The less time we spend on it, the better."

Tucker found the rhythm of the sloshing waters to be soothing as they carried him into the night. As Manaloul had predicted, the water seldom reached his waist. It had remained fairly consistently at about knee-level. The sky was dark and starless as Tucker felt the first sign of the dry land. By dawn the swamp gave way to miles of tacky mud before turning solid with hardened trails blanketed in pine needles. In the dawn's dim light, Tucker watched as the green walls of Neveria ended, and the gray tangles of leafless branch began. All he saw was colorless clusters of branch and thorn. Deadwood Pass was a lifeless place, cold and barren. Tucker fought off the cold, and he stopped along the path to rest. He crouched next to the roadway and propped himself against a large trunk of rough colorless bark.

"This place is so cold and lifeless," he told Treol.

"Legends say the pass is enchanted, charmed by a fairy who lost a loved one to the creatures dwelling in the dark," Treol replied.

"The wind howls of pain and sorrow," Tucker agreed. "My legs ache from walking. I need to rest."

"We need to keep moving. It is unwise to rest in Deadwood Pass. Devious spells work the forest. I advise you to bury the leaf, and make your way back toward Neveria to rest."

Tucker reached into his sack and took out the crumbling dried leaf. Its brown cracked shell enhanced branches of veins that snaked across the four-pointed leaf. Tucker knelt to the ground and dug a crevice into the dry soil with the edge of a nearby stone. The soil below the surface was not unlike the dry, crumbly, gray ground on which he had walked. He put the leaf into the crevice, then he quickly pressed the chunk of soil he had removed back into place. After a few well placed taps with the stone's edge, the ground looked as it had before the disturbance. Tucker blinked a few times, then he rubbed his tired eyes. The entire pass was drab and without color. There were no calls from morning birds, no chirps from restless insects. There was only the still and the echo of faint wind through covering of bare tree limbs.

"There," Tucker said as he returned to his feet. "The leaf has been buried in the soil of Deadwood Pass as Manaloul requested. Let's hurry back to the comfort of Manaloul's dwelling."

Before buttoning his knapsack, Tucker took a refreshing swallow of clear water from one of the skins and nibbled on some of the salted fish. Treol took a crumb for himself as they turned to begin their way back toward the wetlands. There was a soft rumble, then a tiny quake Tucker felt through the bottom of his feet. Then the pattern repeated. That caused him to turn and take out his wand in a single motion. Directly behind them, in the spot where the Leaf of Autuine had been buried, there arose a gate of twisting vines and thorny briars. The center was open and revealed a clear view to the leafless forest behind the trestle.

"Treol, it's a gate!"

The Forest Farrow sprang to attention and strained for a clearer view from Tucker's pocket.

"A gate to where?" Treol asked.

"I don't know, but I suppose Manaloul meant for us to pass through it. Just be at the ready. I am reluctant to venture into unknown magic like this."

Tucker cautiously approached the trestle that hovered several feet above the top of his head. He paused and took a deep breath before stepping through the center of the opening. There was a brief flash of light, and then his foot came down on the forest floor on the other side of the gate. The forest looked the same at first, but there was color. The leafless trees were alive with hues of yellow and orange. Leaves tumbled like rain in the warm breeze and gathered on the ground in giant piles. The pass was alive with sounds of birds singing morning songs from branches above, and several deerlike creatures took notice of Tucker and raised their heads from a silvery stream from which that they had been drinking.

"What happened, Treol? Where are we?"

Before his companion answered, the voice of a female spoke from behind.

"Welcome to Autuine," it said as Tucker spun around in surprise.

Treol held his arrow tight against the string of his bow.

"There is no need to raise your weapon here. You will find you are in good company, King of Zooblatia."

At first sight she appeared to be a human woman, taller than he and slender with wisps of thin hair that danced gently in the breeze. As she approached, Tucker's view became clearer. Her hair that he thought was auburn, was actually streaked deep purple, and on her back were four giant wings that were nearly invisible from every angle, and transparent.

"Who are you?" Tucker asked.

"Do not be afraid. I am Cherya, keeper of the Gate to Autuine."

"Where are we? Are we no longer in Deadwood Pass?"

The stranger frowned.

"Do you not recognize this place? It is as the world once was. The lands were laid to sorrow by the spells of my kindred. They appear cold and lonely to the eyes of travelers now. Autuine became a wasteland devoid of life to all eyes, and was renamed by the Zooblatians as *Deadwood Pass*."

"So the legends then are true," Treol mumbled to himself.

"What can we do to break the spell?" Tucker asked.

"Some paths cannot be unmade by virtue of task alone," Cherya said softly. "There are many things you do not understand. I will try to enlighten you if I can."

"I am weary from travel," Tucker said. "I fear my mind is clouded. How can I be certain I have not drifted into a dream?"

"First, rest before we continue, traveler. You will find sleep in the shade of the Autuine trees to be replenishing."

Tucker sat in a pile of golden leaves that accumulated at the base of a giant tree. The leaves offered a cushion that took him by surprise. He didn't resist the overwhelming sensation to lie flat on his back. He watched as orange leaves danced slowly downward. Exhaustion washed over his limp body. Heavy eyelids pulled him into the warmth of slumber.

The line between dreams and consciousness was thin. Tucker could find no recollection of waking. Instead, he found himself rising to his feet while Treol slept peacefully in his pocket. Cherya was standing near, singing a song in which her words became lost with the breeze. In what tongue she sang Tucker did not know, but the beauty of the words was as delicate as the leaves. She said nothing. Tucker followed her up a gradual slope that came to a shady plateau. It was there Tucker noticed a table of white iron scroll that did not seem out of place, even in an area so desolate. He took a seat across from Cherya. She poured sparkling nectar from a clear crystal pitcher into two tall glasses.

"You are here," she began, "because the path of the throne of Nespa' has gone dim to our ever-watchful eyes. The peace of Zooblatia is once again in jeopardy."

Tucker sipped the sparkling nectar from his glass. It was warm and soothing, like the very air itself, and like the sounds, and like the trees.

"Young king," she continued, "Zooblatia is older than you realize, older than the land from which you have come. For many ages the lands were divided, leaderless, and without hope. Fairies, like my forbearers, were appointed the task of governing the war torn lands because of our discipline, our love for all living things, and our abilities as healers. The task was overwhelming, and we witnessed the destruction of a once peaceful and loving people. The fairy way was never one of violence, aggression, or destruction. We strove to share the peace of our race with all. We failed."

Tucker took another sip of the nectar. He felt the warmth of it in his cheeks, then swallowed it slowly. It was soothing and it made his body tingle from his fingers down to his toes. At the same time, it sharpened his senses. He could almost hear comforting voices humming in the breeze.

Night Of The Stalkers

"Our time as rulers passed at the will of the Wyvern and the first appearance of the Crystal Stone that smashed into fragments from the skies above, poisoning an already tattered land with a new form of greed. We thought if the races of Zooblatia had a common symbol to unite them, true and lasting peace could be established. We distributed the crystal fragments, initially. Our intentions were pure, to create a common ground in which all could share. The crystal fragments were more than a symbol. They were hope to a land with no hope. We thought they to have no power of their own, but discovered the alien rocks reacted adversely to our atmosphere. They appeared untarnished at first, clear and pure. It wasn't until they were distributed that the truth became clear. The fragments were superconductors of emotion. They were quickly tainted and dimmed with color. It didn't take long for the honest to begin to use the crystals that had been given them for good. It was with equal haste that the Wyvern and the Night Stalkers channeled ill intent. What followed was the darkest recorded ages of Zooblatia. Wars raged throughout the lands. The power of the crystals magnified the range of destruction. Most of my people were destroyed trying to take back the crystal fragments. The Fairy Kings of Losparia were assassinated. Those of us who remained were forced to flee. We have remained in hiding in Autuine ever since."

"The spell on Deadwood Pass exists to protect you?"

Night Of The Stalkers

"Yes. However, we are prisoners here, forced to endure the ages from behind a veil. Our influence has been rejected, and so our will places us here in a time and place all our own. The only way back to Autuine for you is by planting one of our eternally golden leaves in Deadwood, a secret held by very few."

"What if you were to cross back over into Zooblatia with me?"

"We are no longer able to pass through the Gate of Autuine. The power of our broken will has sealed it permanently on our side of the gate. There are turbulent currents of power and unbalance endlessly ripping through Zooblatia. There are struggles of scattered energy as the crystals attempt to balance. We are victims of the power we carelessly distributed long ago. The imbalance of the crystals keep us here indefinitely."

"You are forced to remain here forever?"

Cheerya slowly nodded.

"We had our chance. We failed to restore peace to Zooblatia. Raymond Harvey took up our thrown. You are his successor. Our only hope is with you, that the throne of Nespa' can succeed where we have failed."

Tucker debated whether he should tell her Losparia had been destroyed, that the senate was no longer, that he was a refugee, and that the Night Stalkers were suspected behind the acts. Before he could speak, the sweeping sensation he was falling washed over him. He dropped onto his hands and knees and spilt the remaining nectar in his glass. He clutched a single fallen leaf in his hand. The humming stopped, and the air grew colder. He blinked several times as darkness fell around him and the sounds of the forest were replaced by heavy silence. He felt the cold bark of the gray knotted tree in Deadwood Pass pressed against his back. He sat up. Was it a dream? Treol stood next to him, worried about his companion.

"We should get moving Tucker," he softly whispered. "It isn't wise to linger in Deadwood."

Tucker was confused and dizzy. He opened his left fist and found the golden leaf whole in the palm of his hand. He slipped it into his knapsack and scooped Treol up into his hands. It was a long walk back to Neveria.

CHAPTER EIGHT

Reunited

The gray light of early dusk filtered through the moist green canopy of Neveria as Tucker approached the hillside. He managed to stay on a tighter course for the return trip. He splashed loudly through the water as he approached. The hidden hatch of green moss and tall grass flipped open and revealed the hooded head of Manaloul.

"Hurry, hurry lad," he called out waving his hand to guide Tucker into his home.

Manaloul closed the hatch behind Tucker and followed him into his chamber. Tucker sighed and plopped himself onto a wooden chair at the round table in the center of the room. He unfastened the knapsack from his back. Petri immediately flew to perch on Tucker's shoulder. Manaloul hastily lit several lamps, then he sat down.

Night Of The Stalkers

"The situation is more serious than I suspected," he said. "Time is not on our side. I'm afraid the records that remain of the Gold Crystal are very incomplete, yet I did gathered enough information to answer many of our questions. The Golden Crystal is the youngest of all the Zooblatian crystals. It is the only crystal contrived at the hands of the Order of the Crystalline."

"The Order *made* the Golden Crystal?"

"Yes. Among other things, the Order fostered an unnamed rogue alchemist who believed the properties of the crystals could be duplicated in a laboratory. His theories caused great dissension within the Order because the elder members refused to take part in *any* study. The Order split and divided over the practice that, at that point, had produced *two* synthetic crystal samples. The first was the Magenta Crystal. It was stolen by thieves and taken to the Wyvern of the northern wastelands where it was bartered for riches and plunder. Before the production of synthetic crystals was entirely banned, the rogue alchemist managed to develop another unnatural crystal gem. This was the Golden Crystal, and it was intended to reopen the Gate of Autuine."

Manaloul lit his pipe and slowly closed his massive eyes.

"The Golden Crystal was far more unstable than the alchemist estimated. It's powers were met with an unforeseen side effect. In addition to reacting like an explosive when introduced to the effects of the ancient Red Crystal element, it was impossible to control where and when the Golden Crystal would disrupt the fibers of space and time. The Golden Crystal ripped holes in the very fabric of existence, often with devastating consequences. It was seemingly random and quite disastrous. The elders of the Order of the Crystalline banished it from our world. The alchemist was stripped of his allegiance. Deep within the caves of Appelia a final portal was opened through which the Golden Crystal was cast."

Tucker leaned forward. His eyes were wide with excitement.

"That was the portal to my world," he said enthusiastically.

"To your world indeed! However, the Golden Crystal displayed another act of defiance. Once cast through the portal away from Zooblatia the crystal lingered in your world and kept the gate open from the other side. This meant there was no way to close the gate from our side. Worse yet, despite the best efforts of the Forest Farrows to recover it, we did not know where the crystals were in your strange land. The senate decided the caves would be permanently sealed. Then a most unexpected turn of events took place. We had a visitor cross over from the other side. I believe you know of whom I speak."

"Mister Harvey," Tucker said.

Manaloul smiled.

"Raymond Harvey brought hope to these lands once more. He was a new king and the head of the senate in a new era of unity. The rest of the story I believe you already know."

"What happened to the Order of the Crystalline?"

Manaloul hung his head.

"Tragically, they were ambushed and destroyed by the Wyvern shortly after King Harvey's arrival. Word of the Golden Crystal reached the northern wastelands. Greed prompted the great beasts to seek the second synthetic crystal for themselves. They failed because the crystal was already cast from our world. Nevertheless, the Order of the Crystalline couldn't withstand the wrath of the Wyvern. There are few forces in all of Zooblatia that could."

Tucker took a deep breath and allowed himself a moment to absorb all he heard.

"So you believe the Golden Crystal has returned through the gate?"

"It is the only explanation. *How* it returned is more difficult to ascertain."

"Listen," Treol whispered in alarm. "Something stirs beyond these walls. I believe we were followed here."

Tucker grabbed Petri's beak with his fingers before his nervous companion could squawk. Manaloul sprang to his feet, and partially revealed his shimmering green wand.

"The Green Crystal detects danger on our path. We must flee at once."

He quickly snuffed the lamps with his bare gray fingers, while Tucker summoned a blast of water to drown the fire in the hearth.

"There is a secret exit," Manaloul whispered.

He rolled away a round stone at the hearth's side. Beyond was a circular tunnel of darkness that led deeper into the hillside.

Tucker carried Treol and Petri and ducked into the small opening. Manaloul followed. He carefully slid the stone back into place behind him.

"I can't see a thing," Petri cried out.

"We cannot talk until we are certain the danger is behind us," Manaloul said in reply. "Even with light there is little to see here, just keep moving forward until the tunnel meets an iron gate. Move quickly and make as little sound as possible."

Tucker scurried along, half crawling on all fours. The floor took a sudden rise. He heard Manaloul's soft footsteps behind him.

"The disturbance has faded," Treol whispered to Tucker. "Be prepared. The gate is almost upon us."

Tucker squinted. He saw no sign of the gate ahead. The blackness all around them offered no indication of end. He kept his hands out to feel for the iron posts, and slowly came into contact with the cold metal grates. Manaloul approached, allowing some of the green light from his wand to illuminate the tunnel's end. Tucker could see tangles of dense foliage around, on, and through the metal of the grates. After a moment of silent meditation, Manaloul waved his wand and the wrought iron gate swung lowly open. With a low moan the rusty gate pushed forward, foliage and all, and revealed an area of open marsh. The cool night air rushed into the stale warmth of the tunnel.

"There is no sign of movement ahead," Treol softly announced.

Tucker stepped free of the passageway and stepped off the slight embankment into the pool of foul-smelling water. It rushed up to his hips. Petri danced nervously on his shoulder. The shorter, stockier Manaloul also stepped into the water. It reached his chest level.

"Make your way through these waters until the Bridge to Sand Crest is in clear view. We will regroup there."

Before Tucker could protest, his odd looking friend had slipped silently under the dark water of the marsh. With a swirl of current and bubble, he vanished without a trace. Tucker fought the fear that loomed up inside of him when he thought about what lay beneath the dark mudded waters. He began drudging slowly away from the grasslands.

The pace was painfully slow. Each step he took had to be well placed to avoid slippery logs, rocks, and sinkholes. The mud at the bottom of the marsh tried to suction the shoes clean off Tucker's feet as he walked. Although the cold stagnant water was only waist deep, Tucker found its chill astounded him. The night sounds of the swamps filled his ears with a cacophony of chirping, buzzing, and distant howling. He put his head down, charged onward, and pressed further and further away from the security of Manaloul's home. Nearly an hour had passed before Treol alerted him to the distant sight of the bridge. It took all Tucker's strength to pull his tired legs up and onto the slowly rising shore. The marsh slowly gave way to the flooded grasslands where the base of the old wooden bridge started. Even through the darkness Tucker could see the bridge silhouetted against starlight passing through the small clearing in the high above canopy. Thoroughly exhausted and dripping wet from the waist down, Tucker propped himself against a thick wooden post. He slowly rolled his wand between the fingers of his left hand. It sprang to dull life, a weak shimmer of pale white that emitted a steady radiant heat. He let out a long deep yawn and held the wand near his legs. Its heat immediately dried him and forced away the cold.

    Tucker drifted in and out of sleep, and was finally awakened by the splashing of Manaloul's approach from the marsh. He stepped calmly onto the shore and onto the bridge base before the light of Tucker's wand illuminated his robed figure. Behind him was a massive, lifeless shape, blacker than the darkness all around. Tucker raised his wand for a better look. Dragged behind Manaloul was the unmistakable figure of a Night Stalker carcass. Its typically menacing bulk folded limply against itself. Petri gasped, fluttering his green wings.

"The other escaped," Manaloul said in a soft voice.

"Night Stalker," Tucker whispered, "*horrible* creatures."

"I suspect they followed you back from Autuine. They must not have realized it was you, or they would have attacked while you traveled. They are not to be underestimated, even by a spell caster as powerful as you've become. Their spells are basic, mostly combinations of the Red Crystal, but they *do* have mastery over them."

Manaloul rolled the massive carcass down the bank. It splashed loudly into the water. There it floated, face down. With a wave of his glowing green wand, the waters stirred with the shimmer of dozens of silver fish darting below the surface. They swarmed the Night Stalker's body and devoured it with alarming efficiency.

"We mustn't linger here," Manaloul said as he took a step toward the bridge. "Like I said, the other escaped. That means they will return in greater numbers."

"We best be on the move then, I assume" Tucker replied as he followed Manaloul back toward the bridge.

"I am reluctant to have you appear in a public area like Sand Crest. However, the arrival of our enemy means we are no longer safe in the marsh. Perhaps by wearing these cloaks, we can avoid attracting attention to ourselves."

"Fair enough," Tucker said.

"We should not use the bridge, my young friend. It is far too dangerous. The bridge is patrolled by Night Stalkers that flock to the mainland from Nocoule."

He waved his wand and muttered a soft chirping sound into the predawn darkness. After several minutes the grass began to stir. A giant spotted slug with two slowly blinking eyes at the ends of pale stalks broke through the cover.

"A grass slug will get us there quietly," Manaloul said as he climbed onto the creature's back.

Tucker looked at the grass slug reluctantly. Then he finally straddled the animal's long tubular body behind Manaloul. Its skin was cold and slimy to the touch. There was nothing to grab or hold for support. Manaloul continued his odd communication with the creature and sent it slithering forward beneath the massive supports of the wooden bridge. It effortlessly glided over the grass and wetlands at walking speed. Tucker was content with the slow, steady pace of the creature, because a faster speed would have caused him to slide off the slippery surface of the slug's back.

After several hours of steady plodding along, Tucker took out the last of the food reserves. He had enough salted fish for himself and Treol and some stale bread that Petri enjoyed.

Night Of The Stalkers

Manaloul ate nothing and claimed he had friends who would host them when they reached Sand Crest. Tucker felt secure in Manaloul's presence, and the remaining members of the group were fairly content trekking together. Yet, he could not escape the looming sensation of fear that gathered around them. Tucker did not dare look behind due to his uncertainty and fear they were being shadowed by some faceless terror that lurked in silence, waiting to strike. Despite a desperate need for rest, Tucker found he could not sleep.

CHAPTER NINE

Sand Crest

It was late morning when the slug reached the limits of the thick canopy of forest. The light steadily streamed onto the dried paths. The smell of the beach was softly carried to the shade, and gently mixed with the stale air of the marsh to their backs. Tucker found himself oddly excited about returning to Sand Crest. It had been many years since his last visit. Life in Losparia had been desolate and riddled with constant classes, meetings, hearings, and training. In fact, Tucker found he could easily forget he was king, most of the time. His kingdom was becoming more shrouded in mystery with each passing day he spent within the walls of stone. A signature here, an announcement there---his duties nearly eliminated the possibility of venturing deep into Zooblatia. He felt as though he was deliberately being kept isolated from the masses. The terrible events that unfolded before him were a combination of an unforeseen nightmare and the confirmation of a nagging suspicion. Tucker managed to convince himself on many occasions that he was being needlessly paranoid about the feelings of conspiracy that clouded his mind. There *were* pieces to the story that seemed not to fit into place, questions that were dodged rather than answered, and forces that mounted to counter every facet of Tucker's decision making power.

The slug came to a gradual stop before the sand met the rapidly thinning wood-line. Between the heat, the dryness, and the sand of the beach, it didn't appear a creature like the grass slug would stand much of a chance in the environment ahead. Manaloul climbed off its back first. He rubbed the animal's smooth head and made a low ticking sound in his throat. The slug answered with a similar series of sounds. Then he turned away from the beach. Tucker stepped off his back, stretched his arms, and yawned. Treol slept softly in his cloak pocket. Petri looked nervously in all directions.

"We must move swiftly and with purpose through the city," Manaloul cautioned. "Stay cloaked at all times on the busy city streets, and keep your face hooded. We cannot risk you being discovered in an area as well populated as this."

The hike across the beach was slow. It was brutally hot. There was no shade in sight. The waves of the sea crashed noisily on the sand. The party crossed paths with many strange faces. Nomads and traders lurked on the outer rim of the city in small camps and gatherings. The sights and smells of Sand Crest flooded back into Tucker's memory as they neared the outermost row of tents. The cluster of activity stretched beyond his field of vision to a seemingly endless column of tents, banners, traders, and dusty streets. The entire area created a unique sensation that Tucker barely recalled, how he felt on a childhood trip to the local carnival with his parents. The aroma of greasy foods filled the breezy air. There was an odd sense of excitement that refused to manifest itself into a single thought. There was commotion, conversation, and assembly around every corner. Most of the odd looking strangers paid no attention to the two robed figures walking hastily along the roadways. Others gazed emptily as they passed with eyes cold and distant. Tucker could feel the heavily beating heart of Petri on his shoulder. This place felt about as far from the serenity of Losparia as Tucker could imagine.

By late morning they reached the inner depths of the city. They stopped only once for a swallow of cordial. While Tucker kept his complaints to himself, the truth was he had been hoping they would soon arrive at their destination. His feet ached, and his knees felt weak from all the walking. Manaloul was not suffering as he was in this travel in an environment so different from the lands he called home. Tucker wondered if the Swamps of Neveria were Manaloul's native lands.

"We are here," Manaloul said softly as they approached a rounded dome of dried clay.

The structure was featureless on the outside, a sort of crusty beehive with only a single door hatch facing the busy lane. The domed roof was spider webbed with tiny cracks of black. It was dwarfed in size by the neighboring trader tents and endless stacks of wooden crates ready for the nearby docks. Manaloul muttered several quiet words, then he tapped the door hatch twice with the tip of his wand. There was a pause. Then a voice from inside the dome seeped through the clay walls.

"Dark waters, light sand, of clay and mud assembled: Who dare approach my doorstep with heart and mind to enter?"

"From wetland, to rotten wood, to sand, and now to daylight: My voyage may be unannounced, a reply to your invite."

The door slid quickly open and revealed a dark and shady opening amidst the hot afternoon suns.

"Quickly now lad," Manaloul said as he allowed Tucker to enter first.

The air inside the domed hut was cool and dank, a sharp contrast to the fresh warm breeze that washed over them outside. There was a slight musty feel to the darkness, an odor that reminded Tucker of his days living in his parents' basement. Manaloul followed Tucker into the small opening and shut the hatch securely behind them. What little light there was turned to complete darkness.

"Manaloul the Wise," a voice rang out in front of Tucker.

"Chausseur, Battle Cat," Manaloul replied. "How long has it been, old friend?"

The figure ahead of Tucker revealed a lantern that it slowly lit. As the room brightened, the shadow pushed away from the creature's intimidating appearance. Petri squawked and flew to the floor near Tucker's feet. Its appearance was intimidating, and Tucker felt himself instinctively reaching for his wand.

"No need for your weapon here, friend of Manaloul," the stern voice said. "I believe you'll find we are in league with each other."

The tall muscular form in front of him had a face like a lion with deep green eyes that slit in the middle like a cat's eyes. It stood upright and wore a suit of silver and red battle armor. Only small sections of the animal's gray and black spotted coat showed through the armor. Its exposed hands ended in razor-sharp curled nails and its tail danced freely behind it, almost as if it had a mind of its own. Behind the creature and below the far wall of the hut was a set of steps leading downward. Chausseur barred the door hatch with a large wooden beam and led the travelers down the steps by light of its flickering lantern. Tucker's initial fear was replaced with a new feeling of confidence in having this stranger as an ally.

The steps wound around and led to an underground assembly area reminiscent of Manaloul's den, except that the floor was covered in furs and soft pillows. Shelves filled with bottles and candles lined the walls, and rich lavish tapestries and flags covered the areas where shelves did not. To the far corner, rather than a hearth or suspended soup pot, was a large weapons rack. Swords of varying lengths, a heavy mace, and a fancily inscribed battle-axe filled the rack. The room was silent and quite comfortable, almost impossibly opposite the environment outside.

"There is a great threat to the peace of Zooblatia," Manaloul began.

"I know," Chausseur responded. "I have seen the winged predators traveling by night to their lands, only to return in greater numbers. They amass a force in secret."

"Tucker, reveal yourself to our friend," Manaloul directed as Tucker threw back the dark hood that had shadowed his face.

Chausseur's green eyes widened in surprise.

"The King of Nespa'," he hissed and bowed in respect. "It is rumored you were destroyed by assassins and the walls of Losparia have fallen."

"It is true Losparia has been destroyed. However, I assure you they didn't manage to assassinate me."

"How is it you traveled so far without being spotted by the spies of the enemy?"

"We have traveled by cover of dark skies," Manaloul answered, "and we have made very little contact with those we encountered."

"There are few who can be trusted, especially in these lands. I owe you my allegiance, your majesty, as one of the remaining members of the Sand Crest army."

"I did not know Sand Crest had an army."

"Oh it did, indeed, back when there was still something for which we felt was worth fighting. The Sand Crest army protected these shores from attack for many years while the Fairy Guardians and Wyvern battled for control. I went into service because of my father who fought to defend Sand Crest during the Crystal War era."

"It is because of these forces," Manaloul added, "that Sand Crest remained neutral during the Crystal Wars."

"Quite true," Chausseur said. "But it is also because of that neutrality that Sand Crest has become a haven for scoundrels, gypsies, nomads, and illegal traders. All of those who did not wish to take a stand in the ancient battles of good and evil found them selves here. Now, I fear all that remains is lawlessness. What forces that *do* live on here are scattered and divided, and have chosen a life of hiding in these old bunkers."

Night Of The Stalkers

"Do you not recognize the Chausseur crest?" Manaloul asked Tucker.

Tucker gazed at the embroidered gold shield emblem on a tapestry near the weapons rack. Across the shield was the shadow of a large cat on all fours silhouetted against the pale moon. Beneath the cat, two long swords crossed. The same crest used to hang in one of the conference chambers in Losparia.

"Long has the Chausseur family defended freedom from outsiders. Even now, this is one of few allies on which we can depend."

The cat bowed its massive head in silent thought.

"Even if I was able to gather all the remaining troops at my disposal, Manaloul, we would be *impossibly* outnumbered against the hordes of Nocoule."

"I know," Manaloul said softly. "This is why we must summon all who *will* come to our aide."

"Who remains to answer our call? The Zoobles have no weapons or defenses. The free races of Sand Crest care of nothing but money. The Sea Dwellers have numbers but can't be trusted. The Fairy Guardians abandoned these lands long ago."

"The Forest Farrows will fight," Treol said, as he exposed himself for the first time since their meeting began.

Chausseur's green eyes fell onto a steely stare in the direction of the tiny warrior.

"Indeed," he said. "If legend of your kind is even partially true, the Forest Farrows aren't to be taken lightly by our enemy. And I see my young king is just full of surprises."

Manaloul paced the room in deliberation.

"What's worse," he said reluctantly, "is I fear the Gold Crystal has returned to Zooblatia."

The Battle Cat froze, a look of distress crept across his bold face.

"Such ill tiding! This is *hardly* an *encouraging* thought in which we may take comfort," Chausseur complained.

"There is only one in whom we can take comfort," Manaloul answered, "and he is standing here before you."

CHAPTER TEN

The Return to Strength

The party stayed with Chausseur for nearly a week in his underground bunker. The Battle Cat managed to summon several dozen members of the ancient army who still resided in the nooks and crannies of Sand Crest. Tucker spent much of his time quietly hiding. He ventured into the streets of the city only at night, disguised in heavy robes. Manaloul and Chausseur endlessly discussed their plan of action and covered the battle's strategies from all angles.

"Tucker," Manaloul said quietly at breakfast on the seventh day, "I'm afraid we are going to have to send a messenger to the Hidden Village to bring word of our desperation to the Forest Farrows."

"I will gladly return to my lands," Treol offered.

"No Treol," Manaloul replied. "You will be more valuable accompanying us on the initial raids. Your keen senses will warn us of enemy traps. I'm afraid Petri will have to handle this task."

"No, please sir," the bird pleaded. "Tucker, please do something."

"I'm sorry my friend. When it comes to such things, Manaloul knows best."

"Follow the shore line," Manaloul told them. "It is the most direct route. You have the protection of the Green Crystal upon you."

"How will I know when I've arrived?"

"The sea will open into a beautiful bay between the western cliff faces," Treol said. "Take this as a symbol to my people, they will recognize it immediately."

Treol tied a scrap of ribbon around the bird's right leg. With a wave of his wand the rope lit to silver sparkling life. Manaloul folded a small patch of yellowed paper into the band and gently pat the jittery bird on the head.

"Your bravery will be remembered throughout the ages."

Tucker smiled.

"I know you can do it, little buddy," he said.

The bird drew a deep breath and noisily fluttered up toward the top room of Chausseur's home.

"I'll find you again your majesty," he cried out. "I promise."

Night Of The Stalkers

"I'm counting on you!" Tucker yelled to the little bird.

The remaining day passed painfully and slowly, because Tucker couldn't shake off the thought of Petri falling into peril. He took slight comfort at the thought of the Forest Farrows' hospitality.

Manaloul returned in the late afternoon with a cart filled with supplies. Tucker glanced at the cart and noticed heavy blankets and hooded cloaks, fresh water skins, tall loaves of fresh bread, and several wrapped packages of cured meat. The thrill of excitement was in the air, an energy Tucker felt slowly building to a crescendo. The hour was approaching. The comfort of the bunker would be left behind. The path into the unknown lay head.

Chausseur hurriedly returned to the bunker.

"I've managed to find us a contact," he said. "We'll be close to thirty strong with a captain and a first mate, so we'll need a fairly large ship."

Manaloul nodded in approval and slowly lit his pipe.

"That should be enough for a strike team. We'll go to the Port of Thieves as soon as we secure the ship."

"The Port of Thieves?" Tucker questioned.

"Yes," Chausseur answered. "It's a tiny trader island just off the coast of the Nocoule. It will be our final stop before we dock at the enemies' doorstep. We'll need to contact Lucinda here in Sand Crest. She is the president of the Trade Committee and a very powerful figure in the Sand Crest underworld. Her headquarters is deep in the center of the seventh lane. It will be well guarded. Seeking her company is by appointment only."

Manaloul sighed.

"Have your crew load our supplies into barrels. We must leave before word spreads of our mission. I will have the ship ready for launch at sunset. We must travel lightly, under dark skies, and by swift current."

Chausseur looked at Manaloul skeptically.

"And if you do not succeed in securing us a ship?" he asked.

"I will succeed. Tucker, you and I will make contact with Lucinda. Chausseur, have our provisions gathered and ready to go by the time I return."

Tucker followed Manaloul through the maze of the midday congestion on the streets of Sand Crest. They hooded themselves again, so no one could see their faces. As Chausseur told them, a sprawling heavily guarded tent occupied most of the seventh lane. Manaloul approached the front entrance. Twin guards locked heavy pikes before their path.

"Let me handle this," Manaloul told Tucker. "Wait for my cue."

"This area is off limits," one of the guards said coldly. "Turn around and go about your business."

"We have come to speak with Lucinda," Manaloul told them.

"Nobody sees Lucinda without an appointment, especially not a pair of vagabond peddlers," the guard explained as the other guard snickered under his breath.

"Then we would like to make an appointment."

The guard rolled his eyes. He was clearly irritated.

"Come back in two weeks," he said. "If she's here in Sand Crest when you return, we'll grant you a moment to speak with her. Be gone with the both of you!"

The pair turned and headed back into the street. Tucker felt a soft jab in his side. He fingered his wand, and then waved it as well as he could beneath the loosely flowing robes. A small focused gust of wind pushed against the upper level canvas of the massive tent popping free several support stakes driven into the sand. A large section of the tent filled with air, floated up and flapped loudly in the breeze.

One of the guards said, "We'll have to get the others and lock that down."

Tucker turned as the guards vanished into the shadowy entrance.

"We make our move now," Manaloul said as he waved to Tucker to follow him into the newly opened hatch in the rear of the tent. They ducked quietly through into the cool shade of the massive structure. The interior was divided into many partitions. Large open rooms were separated by long tunnels. Led by the green sheen of Manaloul's wand, they were whisked along the dim canvas corridors until they arrived near the central chamber. Another set of armed guards faced the intruders. Manaloul slid to a halt just shy of the reach of their pikes.

"How did you get in here?"

"We are here to speak with Lucinda," Manaloul said.

"Nobody speaks with Lucin," the guard began before a loud voice rang out from the room beyond.

"Who is it?" the voice asked.

'Two traders, it would appear, although I've never seen them before," the guard replied.

"Admit them after you've searched them for arms."

The guards frisked them by giving their robes a rough pat-down. Either they did not detect the wands, or they did not realize they could be used as weapons. Manaloul led Tucker into the dimly lit main chamber. There was a burning torch in each corner of the room, and red fabric hung across the interior canvas, casting an eerily alien world of shadow upon them. Lucinda lay motionless in the center of the room, a massive furry spider, with legs tucked tightly to a segmented body. She stood as they entered, and rose to twice the height of a grown man. She wore bands of gold studded gems on each of her eight furry legs. Her head, disproportionably smaller than her body segment, glistened with gem piercing. Manaloul bowed in respect and signaled for Tucker to do the same.

"Time is money," the spider said impatiently. "Money is time. I wonder how much this audience will cost me."

"We will be brief," Manaloul said.

"You are spell casters," she interrupted. "Had I known this, I would've had my guards capture you so that I could feast on your liquid innards."

"Lucinda," Manaloul said, his voice confident and stern, "we wish to bargain with you for use of a supply ship."

"Straight to the point," she hissed." I admire that in a trader."

"We are not traders," Manaloul said. "However, we do seek passage to the Port of Thieves."

Tucker noticed the spider was interested after she heard their destination.

"The standard fee for chartering a merchant ship is four thousand silver pieces in advance, and another hundred silver pieces for each day of use."

"We cannot pay this," Manaloul said. "However, we would be willing to run a shipment to the Port for you in exchange for use of the boat."

The spider laughed and turned away from them.

"The payment for a delivery run is less than the cost of the lease of my ship. I do not know what Crystal Magic you cast stranger; however, it has little effect in making logic out of madness."

Manaloul hung his head in defeat.

"Very well then," he conceded.

"Wait! Perhaps you *could* be of some use to me. I will let you use a ship from my fleet, but *not* because I am concerned with the welfare of you or of your quiet friend. You see, I've had four ships in the past month set sail to the Port of Thieves only to have them never return. I will allow you to set sail in exchange for information regarding the failure of my ships to return."

"We are filled with gratitude," Manaloul said.

"I fear you will suffer the same fate as the sailors who set forth before you," she said as she wheeled around to face them. "They were more likely than not destroyed by the sea."

"Are you sure they didn't *steal* your ships?"

"I am *quite certain* they knew *drowning* was the *only* acceptable alternative, to not returning my ships."

On the walk back to Chausseur's bunker, Tucker looked at Manaloul with a deepened sense of admiration.

"I sense less fear in you," he said to Tucker. "You have become hardened to the ways of battle."

"I am not afraid, Manaloul, not of battle."

"You have seen Cherya. I feel her strength in you. She has given you new hope."

Tucker nodded.

Night Of The Stalkers

"Autuine was one of the loveliest places I've ever seen. My memory of it is like a wonderful, distant dream."

"In the Fairy tongue, Autuine means Eternal Autumn. These lands were different when the Guardians had control. The splendor has been stripped away by ages of war and destruction."

"Why didn't anyone tell me the throne of Nespa' belonged to the Fairy Guardians? This was never mentioned in any of the training and instruction I've received."

"A lot of the past was lost to rumor. You were not ready to learn the truth. This truth needed to come directly from the source to be fully understood."

"She told me the crystals would destroy the Guardians if they returned."

Manaloul exhaled a steady stream of gray smoke that curled lazily upward in the late afternoon sun.

"They hold themselves responsible for the distribution of the crystal fragments. However, none so fair should be bound to this sentence. Alone, the crystals are powerless. They are mere channels of energy. The Fairies, in their innocence, were above their influence. They chose to share the rare elements with all of Zooblatia. They were to be gifts of beauty and symbols of unity. It wasn't until after the crystals were distributed that their secrets were revealed. By then the damage was done."

"So they chose exile?"

Night Of The Stalkers

"Forced into it they were, by the imbalance of power that the crystals had created. The Wyvern evil became more powerful than the Fairies could wrest. The line of Nespa' was broken and remained an empty throne until Raymond Harvey's arrival."

"He was the first human to inherit the throne?"

"Yes. The races of Zooblatia would never allow another of themselves to rule. Humankind was unbiased, neutral to the power struggles. King Harvey made many decisions in his rule. He put an end to criminal cartels like Phoso's Black Moon that had been running rampant in the cities. He opened free trade to Sand Crest. He was in the process of negotiations with The Port of Thieves when his reign came to an early end."

"But my succession had little real power. I mean I was king, but it seemed like the senate made all of the decisions. I don't understand what purpose the king actually serves."

'It troubles me to say it, but I believe the senate took advantage of your youth. I suspect that they used you as a living symbol of freedom. A successor to the throne of King Harvey wouldn't dare be threatened by the enemies of democracy. It appears as though their plan would have been successful if these ambushes had not occurred."

"I don't understand what is in it for the Night Stalkers. I saw to it they were handsomely rewarded for their services. They had formed a proud army in Zooblatia."

Night Of The Stalkers

Manaloul puffed his pipe thoughtfully.

"That is beyond the reach of even the Green Crystal, my lad. I'm afraid there is some other force behind their recent attacks. Its identity is clouded from me as are its intentions. I can only hope traveling to Nocoule will bring us answers."

Chausseur greeted them outside his home flanked by twenty battle clad warriors. Tucker recognized the muscular figures immediately. They were the pig-like creatures he encountered long ago in Deadwood Pass. They wore helmets made of thick brown hide that showed only their stubby tan horns. Their beady yellow eyes were covered in shadow, while their turned up snouts and tusks were visible through their armor. They carried large battle-axes and maces. On their backs were broad shields baring the Chausseur Family crest.

"Manaloul," Chausseur cried out, "did your meeting end with favor? My troops are assembled."

Manaloul knelt to the sandy ground, snuffing out the ashes from his pipe.

"The hour is at hand!" he shouted in reply. "It is as I have foreseen. There will be blood lost on this night. Let us hope it is not ours."

CHAPTER ELEVEN

The Port of Thieves

The horizon ahead changed very little throughout the night. Tucker found it impossible to sleep aboard the rocking ship. The pig warriors, Graindas, as they were called, took turns standing guard throughout the night. Tucker's quarters were below deck. Across the hall in the war room, Chausseur and Manaloul continued plotting until just before dawn. Manaloul told Tucker they would be at sea for a full day before arriving at the Port of Thieves.

"We can expect a warm welcome there," he said. "The Port is home to many free traders and peaceful sea dwellers. The Armies of Sand Crest and the free people of the Port of Thieves shared peace for many years."

Sea sick and beyond overtired, Tucker stumbled up to the main deck shortly after dawn. The coast of the Zooblatian mainland was behind them, and nothing but blue emptiness spilled out ahead. He felt a surge of vertigo as he panned a full circle with nothing to see in any direction except endless choppy waves.

He walked to the rear of the massive wooden vessel and looked over the side of the boat to gaze at the mesmerizing white foam of the ship's wake. For a moment, he convinced himself he'd spotted a glimmer of blue scales below the gray water's surface. He surmised it was a Sea Dweller near the surface, returning to the depths of the sea. Tucker took comfort in imagining it was old friend Oso, patrolling along side the ship as an underwater escort. The steady bobbing combined with memories of time he and Oso spent together tired him. He returned to his quarters where he fell asleep.

Despite Treol insisting it was still late afternoon, the sky appeared dark when Tucker awoke.

"We are close to our destination," Manaloul said as Tucker approached the main deck.

On the distant horizon, the sky appeared pale red, like the midsummer sunset above the lake Tucker remembered from his childhood. Only here, the light of day was still behind them. Thick black clouds rose in columns into the scarlet sky. The ship banked slowly, hooking slightly away from an unknown, impending doom ahead. Then it leveled out until a tiny spec appeared on the horizon, a darkened silhouette against the menacing sky.

"That is the port!" Chausseur announced.

"Why is it called the Port of Thieves?" Tucker quietly asked Manaloul, hoping the Grainda guards wouldn't overhear him.

"Because of its close proximity to Nocoule, it has become a resting spot for smugglers and pirates. Very few soldiers are brave enough to follow a vessel into these parts."

"Bring her about," Chausseur said as he motioned for his troops to begin lowering the massive sails of the ship.

The port was smaller than the Sand Crest port. In fact, it appeared defenseless and alone amidst a horribly uninviting backdrop. The ship worked its way into the bay where the gentle currents pulled it into a docking area that was still and silent. Two Grainda Guards leapt onto the dock below and began securing the ship with heavy braided rope. Manaloul meditated quietly for a moment. His wand illuminated pale green. Treol put his bow and quiver over his shoulder, and he took his position in Tucker's cloak while Chausseur sheathed his long sword.

"No welcoming party to greet us," the tall muscular cat commented under this breath. "These docks are usually home to many beautiful ships."

"I fear there is very little activity in the city," Treol quietly answered. "The stillness is very unusual."

"We need to stick together and be on guard," Manaloul said, returning to the moment as his wand quickly dulled.

Night Of The Stalkers

The crew walked a creaky wooden plank that one of the Grainda had positioned into place from the dock below. The air was warm and stale, nothing like the fresh sea breeze that rippled across Sand Crest.

"Look!" one of the Grainda shouted as it pointed beyond the docks. "They've been attacked!"

Tucker squinted to see for himself. Under the darkened sky in the hazy distance, he saw flattened tents and smoldering huts. The village was silent and disturbingly calm. Chausseur leapt from the plank and landed softly onto the deck. He motioned his troops to follow, then he dashed off into the village. His Grainda followed closely, their hoofed feet pounded the wooden docks in unison. The metallic twang of swords unsheathed and shields swinging into position filled the air with their sounds. Tucker followed behind the lead pack. Only Manaloul was behind him.

"If the attackers still lurk here, I will take you back to the ship," Manaloul told him. "You are far too important to us for us to risk losing to battle."

"But," Tucker interrupted ready to argue.

"No arguments, lad! Our work is *far* from done."

Tucker grew out of breath keeping up with the Grainda's swift stride onto the bank and down the grassy hill leading to the village. As they drew closer, the extent of the damage was sickeningly clear. Slain Sea Dwellers, Adacore, and spider merchants lay scattered about the lanes. Residential huts smoldered and crackled with red-hot flame, while jagged pieces of torn tent floated aimlessly among the cinders. Chausseur knelt to the ground. His wide feline nose sniffed the air. His eyes closed tightly. The Grainda warriors stuck their long swords into the soft soil and bowed their heads in silence. One reached down and then returned to its feet holding the lifeless body of a Night Stalker. Its mass nearly doubled the muscular body of the soldier's. It was a massive black furred bat-like creature, hideous and twisted. The soldier dropped the corpse to the sandy ground.

"It is as I feared," Manaloul muttered to himself. "This attack removes the little doubt left in me."

"No!" Chausseur cried out while he returned to his feet. "No!"

He flipped through several layers of smoldering ash and burnt walls with his claws. The Grainda stood by helplessly watching their leader struggle violently through the rubble. Finally, the giant cat stood up, slinging the lifeless body of what could have been his twin across his shoulder.

"Tucker," Manaloul said softly, "we should return to the ship. There is nothing more to see here."

"Who was that, Manaloul?"

"That was Chausseur's cousin and only living relative. He was also a member of the Sand Crest army, stationed here at the port."

Tucker turned to follow Manaloul back toward the docks. A painful vision raced across his mind.

"Manaloul!" he called out. "There's something wrong here!"

Manaloul continued to walk toward the boat.

"What do you see, my lad?"

"There is a snowy mountain in the distance, and a battle is raging below it. There is pain and suffering. I am holding something in my hand. I do not recognize it."

"It is the future you see."

The vision faded into Tucker's memory as quickly as it had appeared.

"The future?" Tucker asked.

"Yes. The future has yet to be manifest. It is the power of the Green Crystal working through you."

"But I was never taught the ways."

"What wisdom and power are given to me by the crystal's presence, I am beginning to transfer onto you. If I fall without transference, my young king, the Green Crystal's secrets would be forever lost."

"Manaloul, what causes you to fear such things? You can't die."

"I wish that were true. All that is temporary must reach its end. It is the way of life. From the time we enter into existence we begin drawing a set number of breaths. Death is not to be feared. It is to be accepted as a natural part of the life process."

"But master, let us flee from this place if you have foreseen only doom! Return to your home where you'll be safe."

Manaloul stopped in his tracks.

"To flee from one's destiny is not a choice one gets to make. We have a duty to fulfill that which has been appointed to us. There is far more than doom that awaits us on Nocoule."

From behind him, Tucker heard the ignition of a massive pyre. The Grainda snorted, grumbled, and tossed lifeless bodies into rolling flames. Chausseur stood before the roaring monument, a silhouette of darkness against intense light, filled with sadness.

"It begins in the lands closest to their homes, then it spreads outward in all directions. The Night Stalkers are organized and have an attack strategy. They began with Losparia because they knew that a scattered Zooblatia would have no chance of uniting against them. I fear Sand Crest will be next."

"What can we do, Manaloul?"

"Our plans to regroup and refresh our supplies at this port need to be changed. I'll have to contemplate our next course of action."

Night Of The Stalkers

"Wait!" Treol squealed as he climbed up Tucker's shoulder for a better look. "Wait! Listen! They are coming! More Night Stalkers approach from the west."

"Are you certain?" Manaloul calmly asked.

"I am certain."

"Chausseur!" he yelled out. "They're coming!"

CHAPTER TWELVE

The Battle Plan

Treol returned to Tucker's cloak pocket to retrieve his bow as Tucker and Manaloul dashed toward the docked ship. Chausseur and his troops broke the crest of the gray sand dunes and followed in formation onto the wooden dock.

"We must protect the ship," Manaloul said. "We'll form a perimeter here."

Chausseur agreed.

"We draw the line at the edge of the sand. Let no one pass onto the docks."

The Grainda snarled and snorted in anticipation as they faced the dunes with their weapons drawn. Drool ran from their tusks in long clear strings. Tucker felt a surge of dread that rushed across his body and sent his stomach into knots.

Night Of The Stalkers

"Control your fear," Manaloul calmly whispered. "Focus on what you've learned and wear your hood. Let not the eyes of our enemy gaze upon the king they failed to destroy."

Blinded by the light of the expanding pyre, Tucker struggled to catch a glimpse of the group of Stalkers that sailed silently through the darkened skies. Tucker flipped his hood up over his head as Treol pulled back on his bow. With a twang of the string, he sent a tiny arrow sailing overhead. After a moment of silence, his arrow exploded into a star of raining silver sparks high above the dunes. In that instant of intense flash, Tucker saw the giant shadowy forms move rapidly towards them. There were at least a dozen of them. The Grainda stomped their hooves loudly against the docks.

"Steady," Chausseur said from the front of the line. "Wait for my command. Let not our nerves thrust us into battle."

Treol pulled another arrow onto the string of his bow. Manaloul gripped his wand in concentration. Tucker unleashed *his* wand. It felt cold against his sweaty palms, but it was comforting and familiar. He closed his eyes and allowed himself to drift into the memory of days in Losparia, of the training he received. The chaos of the fear that welled up inside him was eased by newfound confidence. He felt his wand charge with energy.

He opened his eyes as the first wave of Night Stalkers landed on the top of the dunes before them. Backlit from the pyre, they looked like shadows with red wands glowing. There was a moment of silent standoff that seemed to last for an eternity before the first ball of fire rolled from the red wands and sailed towards them. Tucker watched the rolling ball of fire smash into the waiting shields of the front line. Then the world resumed its normal pace, and the chaos of battle erupted.

Treol's arrows ripped continuously through the heavy air, striking some of the massive bodies with a flash of silver followed by a puff of rising smoke. Fire and blasts of hot energy sailed randomly overhead. Some blasts smashed into the docks. Other blasts hit the ship. The ship began to burn. Tucker waved his wand and focused a blast of wind and water from the sea up onto the vessel's side, extinguishing the flames. The Grainda pushed steadily forward from behind their shields until close enough to their attackers to unleash their brutal counterattack. Axes and long swords swung violently into the melee as fur covered arms and heads lobbed freely into the air. Several Stalkers took to flight and sailed over the battle toward Tucker and Manaloul. Treol continued his barrage. Manaloul blocked the fire blasts on the approach with a blinding flash of green light while Tucker unleashed a flurry of upward wind. The creatures tumbled backward. One lost its wand in the blast. Treol got another with a well-placed arrow that struck right between its evil beady eyes. The Stalker moaned in anguish and tumbled from the dock into the water below.

Night Of The Stalkers

Tucker was distracted by the awful squealing of a Grainda soldier who flailed hopelessly, completely engulfed in flames. Chausseur threw his sword end over end until it struck cleanly through a Night Stalker's chest. He ran to the dying Stalker before it fell. He removed his sword and flailed it blindly toward another Night Stalker behind him. He caught the creature's wand. A shower of orange sparks fell to the ground from Chausseur's blade. Tucker summoned another wave of wind and pushed a nearby Stalker off the dock.

"Push them back," Manaloul cried out.

One Night Stalker took flight as it snatched a pair of Grainda warriors by the shoulders with its trunk-like legs and carried them high above the smoldering trees. They were released to tumble to their fates against the rocks.

Manaloul unleashed a deafening crackle of green energy from his wand and sent the stunned Night Stalker tumbling to its death behind the Grainda it dropped. Axes and swords clashed. Balls of fire and black dust were everywhere. Chausseur pounced on the back of one of the Stalkers and snapped the creature's neck, before back flipping and catching another in flight with his exposed claws. Before the dust settled, several more waves of Night Stalkers came. They landed in even rows all around the battle.

"We're clearly outnumbered!" Manaloul cried. "Fall back Chausseur! Have your troops fall back!"

Night Of The Stalkers

Chausseur gave the command as he continuing to take out one Night Stalker after another in his retreat. Another Grainda flew through the air, covered in flames. It hit the dark water below with a loud splash. The remaining Grainda huddled together with locked shields and retreated slowly to the boat. Fireballs rained down upon them. Some crashed down on top of the troops. Others were deflected harmlessly off their shields. Chausseur leapt over the barricade and ducked his head as Treol's arrows sailed into the cluster of Night Stalkers.

Manaloul followed Tucker up the plank. The surviving Grainda troops each marched up backwards behind the protection of their shields. When the last one made it safely onto the boat, Chausseur threw the plank at the Stalkers, then pounced up onto the main deck.

'Release the ropes!" he ordered.

The Night Stalkers regrouped and began simultaneous flight. The air was filled with the flapping noise of their large leathery wings. Fireballs rained down on the deck. The dried planks were set on fire by the contact. Chausseur acrobatically climbed the mast and released the main sail with a slash of his claws. Balls of fire and smoke continued to fall and strike the exposed vessel.

"Tucker, we'll need a stiff gust of wind to get moving! I'll cover you!" Manaloul shouted.

Night Of The Stalkers

Amidst the confusion and chaos that surrounded them, Tucker closed his eyes and cleared his mind of all distractions. It wasn't long before he could feel the stale air around him. With his hands trembling with adrenalin, he channeled his attention to the wand, and he sent a gust of wind that crashed against the limp sail. Treol launched a steady succession of tiny arrows into the cluster of dark attackers. The ship was thrust from the dock, but it began to lose speed the moment Tucker's spell ended. The Grainda cried out with fury as they threw their heavy spears skyward.

"We'll need another blast of wind!" Manaloul directed. "I'll focus on extinguishing these fires."

Tucker tried once more to move his thoughts away from the battle, to channel the power of the White Crystal. His focus was shattered when a burst of flame and heat crashed down in front of him. The young king slid across the burning deck. Treol, who was thrown free from the explosion, sprinted over to his friend.

"Are you okay your majesty?" he asked.

Tucker attempted to regain his senses.

"I think I'm alright," he said as he allowed Treol to return to his post within the cloak pocket.

Through the flame and smoke that filled the air, Tucker heard the horrible creak of the ship coming apart. He quickly stood to his feet as the middle portion of the ship began to rise toward the evening sky. Loose ropes and burning planks spilled in the direction of Tucker at the bow of the ship. The floor flooded with cold water. The Night Stalkers continued their horrible barrage. A flash of green light followed by the crackle of thunder sent several of them spiraling down into the black waters. Tucker held tightly to the wooden railing as his portion of the ship separated completely from the other half of the ship where Manaloul, Chausseur, and the Grainca remained.

The water rushed up around Tucker. Its cold touch sucked the breath from his lungs. All of his weight was on the railing. Then Tucker felt the wooden fixture snap free from its base as the water reached his waist.

"Treol, hold on!" he cried out as they submerged completely under the cold water.

The chaos of battle was silent and distant the moment Tucker's head slipped below the surface. Through the serenity of the steady rise of stringed bubbles, he could barely see the raining fire or hear the screams of agony. For a moment, it became a dream from which Tucker half-expected to awake. Then just as quickly as he had fallen into the cold water, the section of railing onto which he had been holding came bobbing back up out of the water, directly back to the chaos at hand. Tucker couldn't find the strength to paddle back to the floating pieces of burning ship that remained. The waves bounced him steadily along, slowly away from the wreckage and back to the calmer port waters. He felt Treol breathing against his chest. This filled him with a sense of relief strong enough to allow him to stop resisting the currents. He turned over on his back. His feet and arms still dangled in the cold black water. He closed his eyes. The waves rocked him gently into the darkness of the pain behind his eyes. He struggled to sit up a final time and glanced at the battle several hundred feet away from him. It looked like the world was on fire.

CHAPTER THIRTEEN

Driftwood

Tucker woke shivering in the sand. It was a pale gray morning. The wooden railing washed ashore next to him along with several chunks of the charred ship. Aside from the gentle lapping of the waves on the bay's floating docks, the port was silent and still. Suddenly, Tucker sat up. He realized he no longer held his wand. He panicked. Then he found it sticking out of the sand a few steps from the edge of the water. His clothes were soaked and heavy with sand that was packed up on his clinging robes. Treol appeared on the crest of a nearby dune and scurried over.

"Treol, the ship's gone."

The tiny Forest Farrow nodded.

"There's not much left out there. The smaller pieces seem to have drifted to shore. Worse yet, the ships docked here must have been sunk during the Night Stalker's first raid. It would appear we're stranded."

Treol looked down at the sand.

"Where are Manaloul and the others?"

Treol shrugged.

"Then we are truly alone here."

Tucker held his face with his hands and sighed. The overwhelming nature of the tragedy had left his mind clouded and his head dizzy.

"We'd better start a hot fire," Treol said, "to get your clothes dry."

Tucker managed a smile. Treol was right as he always was. Before the wave of threatening sorrow could well up inside of him, Tucker reminded himself how grateful he should be to have any companion at all on this gloomy island.

"While we're here, we'll need to get some food," he said.

The fire crackled in the early morning mist and sent a plume of hot sparks skyward. Tucker felt considerably more cheerful as his clothing began to dry. The warmth of the fire reached to his very core. Despite the fact that there was no evidence to support his reasoning, Tucker was certain Manaloul was still alive. His dreams while unconscious had been quite peaceful, playing out before him like scenes from a movie. The Green Crystal was working through him. His visions of the future were becoming clearer and less disrupted by thoughts of the moment.

The Port of Thieves was disturbingly quiet. He and Treol's recognizance hike earlier that morning turned up no sign of life, military *or* civilian. The huts and tents that remained were damaged and scarred by the Night Stalker invasion. Nocoule was close. Of this, Tucker was certain. The ominous sky that loomed overhead wasn't as convincing as the feeling in the air around them. There was a stale taste to the morning. Even the scent of death couldn't mask it. A heavy silence that seemed to spill over from the neighboring mainland. Tucker imagined he would become lost to terror if he focused only on the odd loneliness that flowed around them like a cold mountain river in the spring. Yet, the green Crystal was giving them hope and will.

They walked for a great while, and finally came to a neighboring village. With Treol at his side, he managed to obtain fresh loaves from vendor tents, salted meats, and dried root, and even a few skins of sparkling cordial. It appeared the entire village was completely unaware of the port attack.

As Tucker and Treol slowly feasted on the very welcomed provisions, a series of new questions formed in Tucker's mind. Clearly, the Night Stalkers weren't interested in plunder because the treasury still stood. Even some of the slain residents they had uncovered still carried sacks of rubies on their belts. Tucker hadn't really stopped to consider the enemy motive any more deeply than to look at the obvious senate activities in which he was directly involved. Manaloul was certain the initial attack was more symbolic than functional and was a direct shot into the heart of Zooblatia's democracy. Word of the attack had obviously not traveled to areas as remote as the Port of Thieves, or their defenses would have been prepared for the onslaught. Of course, this led him only to suspect their next target would have to be Sand Crest. With Chausseur and his small band of troops dispatched, there would be few to stand up *there* in resistance. Tucker felt ill considering the prospect of returning to the once bustling city to find it in ruin and destruction.

"You know," Treol said, as he chewed on a slab of salted meat, "this place has made great improvements over the ages."

Treol's words brought Tucker back to the present. He had been daydreaming into the mesmerizing pattern of the firelight.

"I'm not sure I follow you."

"Well, like we were told, the Port of Thieves was founded by pirates and illegal traders who knew that the armies of Zooblatia wouldn't dare to travel so close to the Nocoule mainland. However, it has slowly become a respectable place again. As the Night Stalkers became more cooperative, the place began to take on a newly found beauty. It seems like it would have become the next Sand Crest in time."

"I underestimated them, Treol."

Night Of The Stalkers

The Forest Farrow nodded in thought. A loud cackle of thunder rumbled across the cliffs.

"The Night Stalkers are far more powerful than I suspected. I was overconfident from our battles with the Darkor so many years ago. They were scattered, weak, driven by lust. The Stalkers are now deliberate and cunning. I fear our encounter here is only a sampling of the forces massed on Nocoule itself."

"That is without question," Treol said in response. "We've encountered only a small scouting battalion here at the port. General Garrut's inner sanctum is located in the heart of the mainland. It is rumored it is a sick and twisted land of darkness, ancient and loaded with traps and secret places."

'I wish I knew more about Manaloul's plan of attack. He couldn't possibly have expected our small band of troops to fight well against the armies of Nocoule on a head-on assault."

"No, no. He is certainly far more strategic than that. I overheard Chausseur telling Manaloul that his cousin would join our party once we arrived. He was in command of a couple dozen warriors himself. Perhaps Manaloul intended to recruit here."

Tucker thought for a moment, then nodded in agreement.

"I suspect you're right," he said. "At any rate, you and I are stranded until I can think of someway off this island."

Night Of The Stalkers

Several drops of rain fell upon the calm water, expanding in rings. Then with a perfectly cued lighting bolt, the rain fell in sheets upon the water and the land.

"We better head into the village," Tucker shouted above the steadily pounding rain.

Treol gathered his belongings and darted over to Tucker's waiting hands.

CHAPTER FOURTEEN

Of Prisoners & Refugees

Manaloul turned slowly. His legs were swollen and bruised. His wrists were in shackles that hung from the dripping cave walls by heavy linked chain. Chausseur was to his left, and the lone Grainda survivor, Zarn, was to the left of him. The Night Stalkers seized Manaloul's wand and carried it to the unknown depths of their island. Manaloul's memory of the events leading to his capture was hazy and distant. He knew Tucker had been separated from the rest of the party when the center of the boat buckled and rose upward. The Grainda fought gallantly against their foes to no avail. When the ship went under, they clung to floating scraps of driftwood. Manaloul secured a supply barrel. He paddled over to lift Chausseur from the water. They were struck from the rear. He remembered sinking into the cold dark water, away from the bright flames that lit the surface all around. He recalled a slight feeling that he had survived the battle, and the thought that perhaps he would be able to locate Tucker. Then the world turned dim. What little light remained faded to the darkness of sleep. He woke in this dungeon, presumably hours later. Chausseur was hanging limply from the wall, unconscious, but slowly breathing. Zarn fiddled to loosen his confines and rendered an occasional grunt or sigh of frustration. Around them were skeletons of other prisoners; still shackled by the wrists and ankles with rusty buckles.

"Chausseur," Manaloul whispered, "are you still with me?"

The Battle Cat slowly opened its deep green eyes.

"We failed him," he said at long last, his own voice weak and distant.

"He still lives," Manaloul said. "I can feel him. His presence still reaches out to me from the distance. Fortunately I believe our enemies are not wise to his identity."

"Have they captured him?"

"I don't know. My heart tells me that he has escaped them. I no longer have my wand, so there is no chance for my attempting to contact him. I can channel my thoughts to him, though; perhaps I can be of some guidance to him yet."

"Do you suspect he can follow your thoughts here, to set us free?" Chausseur whispered.

"I'm afraid there will be no rescue party coming for us, my old friend. Tucker's path must lead him to the Gold Crystal and the stranger who wields it. The entire fate of our world lies in his hands now."

Chausseur hung his head and slowly sighed.

"Then our part in this battle for Zooblatia ends here in the darkness of some dungeon long ago forgotten?"

"No," Manaloul replied. "Our roles will still require that we do all we can to aid him on his quest. Our destinies do not lie here with these cold bones."

"We will be tortured and eventually killed," Chausseur said after a long pause. "That is the way of our enemy. They eat the flesh of their victims. . . and *even* their bones."

"And yet, we are surrounded by the bones of those who were left here to die. I do not believe ingesting us is their plan. They are more likely to use us as leverage. As long as we breathe, my old friend, we have a chance."

Tucker wrapped himself in a strip of discarded fabric beneath what remained of the vendor tent they had huddled under for shelter. The rain continued to come down in heavy waves that slapped loudly against the sandy streets outside. The remaining fires were extinguished by the storm. There was little outside of dreary solitude here, and yet Tucker felt strangely optimistic. While he couldn't isolate the exact cause of the hope, he suspected the Green Crystal was playing a part in it. When he closed his eyes, even briefly, he flashed to an image of another island in the setting suns.

Night Of The Stalkers

It was warm and dry with lush green trees that swayed in the evening breeze. He was certain he had never seen the place before, but it was oddly familiar. At times, the vision became so clear in his mind that he felt he could simply explain it to Treol; but each time he tried, the vision scattered like a dream that disappeared with the rooster's crow.

"Treol," Tucker finally asked, "do you know what lies beyond the Nocoule Island?"

"I have never even journeyed this far," he said, "but I have heard there are free lands beyond Nocoule. They are said to be small, probably like this island. I cannot say how many there are or how someone could reaches them. Why do you ask?"

"I have a strange feeling that the land I see in my mind exists beyond Nocoule. There is something or someone there that I am meant to discover."

"How do you know this?"

"I just feel it, Treol. I am becoming more convinced with every passing minute that these visions are the result of the Green Crystal. Its effects are like nothing I've ever felt. It's like a dream that extends across land and sky. It knows no boundary, be it distance or even time."

"Do you see this in the same way you see me standing here before you?"

Night Of The Stalkers

"No. It is quite different. It is more like a feeling or an emotion. The visions are laced with feelings of safety, joy, fear, pain and suffering. This is why I am sure it is the future I see. There are so many paths and so many outcomes."

"Then our fate is already written?"

"No. The visions change with every step I take, with every step you take, with every decision made no matter how minuscule. A vision of joy can turn to fear and a vision of brutal battle can turn into a peaceful field of rye. It is forever-changing."

The Forest Farrow listened intently.

"So you believe we are supposed to try to make our way beyond the Nocoule mainland and onto the open sea beyond?"

Tucker nodded and said, "I know that must sound quite illogical to you. I mean, it sounds foolhardy even to my own ears; but I have a strange feeling that something there awaits us. In fact, I'm certain of it."

"I have known Manaloul the Wise for a long time. His wisdom has never failed my people. If this is the power of the Green Crystal, passed on to you, then I have no reservation about following its guidance wholeheartedly. I will follow you, my king, wherever you decide to lead me."

Tucker smiled. It was good not to be stranded in this foul place, alone. The rain continued to fall. Muddy streams branched out across the roadways.

Night Of The Stalkers

"We should rest here for a while," Tucker said. "Perhaps I'll have a better idea bout what we should do when I awaken."

Manaloul drifted in and out of consciousness. His concern for Tucker carried him in and out of dream. Hours certainly passed, if not days. Chausseur regained his strength in the interim. He stood silently, with his eyes closed in concentration.

"What anger is it that fuels your heart?" Manaloul asked.

The Battle Cat slowly stared blankly forward and inhaled deeply.

"I will avenge the death of my cousin," he whispered in reply. "I defended Sand Crest from our enemy only to have them slaughter free people just outside my patrol. They will not get away with this, Manaloul. I promise you."

"Be calm, my friend. Rushing in to face these beasts will only end badly, with you suffering the same fate as your cousin. I believe enough blood has already been split by the Night Stalkers."

"How can we expect to defeat the inhabitants of Nocoule if not by sheer force?"

"Our young king is on his path, just as the crystal has foreseen. It is as I have told you, our role in this struggle is to offer him what support we can spare. The Night Stalker's failure in allowing him to live is now complete. He will be their undoing, and they know this."

"With the senate destroyed and the walls of Losparia fallen, what is left of the free people of Zooblatia will be scattered and divided."

"I suspect this was their intention all along. We should have been more skeptical at the Night Stalker's willingness to protect our people."

"Did the Green Crystal *not* report to you the deceit in their plan?"

Manaloul shook his head.

"I don't believe they were plotting this course of action all along. There is something elusive in my vision, a veil I am unable to lift. I fear the Night Stalkers are not acting on their own behalf in their raids. Something drives them, or perhaps *someone*. The future is a yet unwritten stream of emotion. The Green Crystal is in tune with what will be on an emotional plane, not a physical one. And so it is that I understood that their actions would one day lead Zooblatia toward harmony. It is just that the events of late are progressing down an unforeseen path and reaching *this* outcome."

"Manaloul do you know what is to become of us?"

Manaloul remained silent. He avoided eye contact with his friend.

"Will you not share with me what the crystal has shared with you? Is our destiny to remain forever in this dungeon?"

"I am reluctant to say too much," Manaloul said after several moments of silent deliberation. "The future has not yet been written other than what is in our hearts at this moment. You must let go of your anger, my friend. It has clouded what could have been passed onto me."

CHAPTER FIFTEEN

A New Plan

Tucker sat beneath the tattered and rain soaked tent fabric. The rain stopped. Heavy gray clouds rolled across the sky.

"Treol," Tucker said as he gently shook his tiny companion. "I know now what we must do."

The Forest Farrow opened his eyes.

'I am certain now that there is an island in the south on the far side of Nocoule that we *must* reach. I saw it all so clearly in my dreams."

"Not with a thousand Grainda could we cross the Nocoule mainland."

"We are not going to cross it. We are going to plot a course around the southern tip."

"But our boat was destroyed. . ."

"We're not traveling by ship. Come, follow me."

Night Of The Stalkers

Tucker stood up and rolled the wet tent back to reveal the cold gray afternoon around them. He pointed his wand skyward, then slowly leveled out its tip to face the westward sea.

"There," he said after a few moments of concentration. "Do your Farrow senses see it yet?"

Treol squinted. A tiny dark object, just a spec in the sky, was approaching.

"You summoned an Adacore?"

"Indeed I have," Tucker said with a smirk. "Our paths will be far less perilous from behind the neck of an Adacore."

"But they rarely fly to these remote reaches. How did you know?"

"I felt its presence, Treol. It was strong enough to wake me from my dream. Let us pack our bags with provisions. This will probably be our last chance to stock up on food and drink. We'll take all we can carry, and load what remains onto the Adacore."

The Forest Farrow looked around.

"Everything here will only go to waste anyway."

Zarn stirred with a series of grunts and snorts that immediately alerted Manaloul. There were light footsteps approaching from one of the deep black corridors in the dungeon. Chausseur also heard it, and his blade-like nails curled in response.

"Don't stir," Manaloul warned in a low whisper. "Let whoever approaches believe that we are not yet awake."

Night Of The Stalkers

Through the darkness, the figure came into view. To their weary eyes, it appeared like a shadow amidst the dark cavern walls. It approached Manaloul first, slinking up quietly. This forced Manaloul to close his eyes in ruse. It breathed heavily on his throat. Then it moved down the line to face Chausseur. Manaloul opened one of his eyes just enough to see the creature make its way to Zarn on the far end of the line. There was a moment of stillness in which all that could be heard was the breathing of the creature and the dripping water from above them. Then it appeared as though the stranger was about to turn away and retreat to the corridors when Zarn let loose an ear shattering squeal that sent the shadow scurrying backward in surprise. It revealed a wand and a small twisted dagger and returned to face the prisoner. Though black and cold, Manaloul recognized the wand immediately as his own. The stranger clearly did not possess the ability to use it, and even more encouraging was that it was almost certainly *not* a Night Stalker.

In the shadow, it drew back its dagger in what appeared to be an attempt to stick the Grainda in the belly, when Chausseur's right arm restraint gave way at the stone-mounted hasp. With a clank of metal links, Chausseur swung the chain so that it wrapped tightly around the shadow. Then he pulled it back to him and sent the stranger tumbling to the ground. Manaloul saw Chausseur's wrist was still shackled to the loosely flying chain.

"Who are you?" Chausseur asked.

Night Of The Stalkers

"I am Oin, keeper of the prison," said a low raspy voice.

"How is it we came to be here, Oin?" Manaloul inquired.

"You were brought here several days ago by a band of Night Stalkers. You were taken captive as criminals against the king. What crimes you have committed they wouldn't say."

"We are guilty of no crimes," Chausseur said in steady and commanding voice. "Release us at once!" he demanded.

"I'm afraid I cannot do that. You were sentenced to death under my supervision."

Chausseur tugged on the chain and rolled the prison-keep over onto his stomach.

"I have nearly snapped my other restraint," he said with a growl. "When I do, I am going to free my companions immediately after I destroy you. If it is a death sentence you insist on fulfilling, I will aid you in seeing it done."

With that there was the creaking moan of another hasp about to buckle.

"No, no," the frightened voice begged. "This is not *my* ruling. I was given instruction from General Garrut himself from the senate. It is my life should I fail to obey the law of Losparia as keeper of this dungeon."

"The Night Stalkers have betrayed and murdered the senate members and have attacked Losparia," Manaloul calmly said. "Your orders did *not* come from the High Court."

Night Of The Stalkers

"Lies!" Oin cried out in pain. "I can't place my trust in lies from guilty prisoners."

The second chain snapped with a loud clank that echoed off the cavern walls.

"You were warned," Chausseur snarled.

"No! No, please I beg you. The Night Stalkers will kill and eat me if I let you go."

"Then I say you have only one choice," Manaloul said as his eyes closed in concentration.

The wand in the shadow's hand began to glow a pale green that grew steadily more intense. At last, it flew free from the creature's grip and sailed end over end through the air into Manaloul's waiting hand. His shackles opened. So did Zarn's.

"You can join us, or you can wait here to explain to General Garrut that we escaped."

The frail looking creature slowly turned over to face them, his eyes wide with fear.

"The choice is yours."

"I will show you the way out," it said at long last. "I don't know if I will join you."

Chausseur broke his wrists free of the shackles. Then he unwrapped Oin from the chain with his free hand.

Night Of The Stalkers

"Be forewarned," Oin said, "the exits to the dungeon are very well guarded. Making it there is only the beginning of obstacles you will face to escape."

Under the glow of Manaloul's wand, the prison guard was finally visible to their eyes. He was small and malnourished and wore only rags for garments. His pale green skin was scarred and scaly. Manaloul recognized him immediately.

"Are you not a Sea Dweller, Oin, prison guard?"

"I was a slave, kidnapped by the Wyvern long ago when I was a child. I do not know my origin or my family. I, along with the rest of the slaves, was traded to the Night Stalkers for gems once the Wyvern became bored with tormenting us. The rest of the slaves were eaten by the Night Stalkers. Why I was kept alive was never made clear. They sent me here to this place underground to keep their dungeon in exchange for scraps of food."

"Your days of being kept as a slave are over now," Manaloul said. "Stand to your feet, Oin. Does it please you to know the Wyvern were destroyed?"

"It does," the Sea Dweller said reluctantly. "But their undoing does little to bring back the innocent lives they took."

Manaloul paused and reflected.

"So true," he said, "sometimes the wisdom of the lowliest is greater than all governments combined. Take comfort in knowing their destruction assures they will no longer spill innocent blood."

"Our weapons," Chausseur interrupted. "Where are our weapons?"

"The weapons the Night Stalkers turned over to me are stored in the armory."

"Take us there," Chausseur demanded without hesitation.

CHAPTER SIXTEEN

Toward Southern Skies

Tucker found communicating with the Adacore had become as natural to him as speaking out loud. He wasted little time in sending the creature into a speedy, updraft driven drift away from the tiny island. The sea below was gray and choppy and stretched out as far as the eye could see in all directions. Tucker did his best to plot a course as far away from the scarlet skies above the Nocoule Mainland as possible, while continuing to approach their southernmost tip. They flew slowly and steadily he first day, using the warm air masses that rose from the water as fuel for the Adacore's massive wings. Treol scanned the area for Night Stalker patrols and kept his keen Farrow senses on high alert, while Tucker continued to base their flight path on the ominous darkness that surrounded Nocoule.

"I know so little about our enemy," Tucker said. "Can you share anything on this subject with me?"

Night Of The Stalkers

"I am afraid my own knowledge of the Night Stalkers comes only from tale and hearsay and will likely be of little use. This is a question that Manaloul could have answered easily for you."

"I do *want* you to share your tales with me, Treol. Your people are wise to the ways of Zooblatia. Surely, they have had much to say on the topic."

"For as long as I can remember, the people of my village warned of the Night Stalkers. Their name comes from their unspeakable habit, sweeping down from cover of night to take live victims back to their homeland. The journey was a horrific experience. The victim dangled limply from the Stalker's talons as the talons were driven deep into their shoulders. It was a flight of several days back to Nocoule. Once there, if still alive from the flight, the victim, weak from lack of food and loss of blood, was devoured whole. Nothing remained in the end, not even bone."

Tucker swallowed hard.

"It is said they feared only the Wyvern themselves and traded with the evil dragons as an alternative to the risk of open war with them."

"That makes sense," Tucker replied. "Once Phoso destroyed the Wyvern, the Night Stalkers positioned themselves as protectors to work their way right into Zooblatia. They managed to amass themselves right under our noses."

Night Of The Stalkers

"The senate should not have trusted them," Treol said softly. "Their history speaks for itself."

"I should have been wiser as well," Tucker said shaking his head. "It was ultimately my vote that got their offer accepted. I suppose my yearning for a united nation blinded me from reason. I was so wrapped up in the prospect of peace that I ended up driving away the very thing I sought."

"But *never* have I heard of them mounting an offensive *like this* on Zooblatia! They were known equally for their cowardice as well as their cunning. They were said to strike alone or in small groups in the dark so as not to risk retaliation. I'm afraid the events of late defy all that my people tell of the Night Stalkers."

"Don't fret, Treol. There is a lot to this mystery that we do not understand."

The wind rippled across the Adacore's feathers as the second sun slowly dipped below the horizon. It had been nearly a complete day of steadily banking on warm air currents beneath the clouded skies. Nocoule's eerie presence, now to Tucker's left, was even more disturbing after sunset. The sky was always scarlet above the mainland, stained with swirls of black volcanic smoke. There appeared endless rolling thunderstorms circling the entire outer region of sea surrounding Nocoule. The air here, like at the Port of Thieves, was heavy and still. Tucker felt almost out of breath at times, even at rest.

Night Of The Stalkers

As the late evening gave way to the blackness of night, Tucker's eyes became heavy from the hours of relentless travel. While no clear words were exchanged, even in Tucker's thoughts, he was certain the Adacore knew the path as it had been given him through his visions. Tucker suspected that perhaps the Green Crystal was partly accountable for the increased sense of understanding that he had been experiencing. It was as if the Adacore needed not even a hint of direction or focused thought to comprehend Tucker's intentions. It was almost as if each crystal skill he had acquired flipped on a light switch to another, previously unknown, room in a darkened house. Tucker began to feel lost and in the dark when he thought back to how incomplete his senses were when he had arrived to Zooblatia. Truly, there was no way to miss abilities one never experienced. But once acquired, there was no going back, of this he was certain.

He willed the Adacore to keep a sharp look out for Night Stalker patrols, especially when he dozed off for a small nap. If encountered, the beast was to dive down from their altitude onto the water's surface to regroup and defend against an aerial assault. In the calm of the early night, Tucker drifted off into a light sleep assured by the fact that his senses revealed no outside presence for miles and miles.

Manaloul and Chausseur followed Oin through endless twisting corridors that wound their way through the deep of the mountainside. Evidently, this entire prison was a partially hollowed out volcano somewhere on the Nocoule mainland.

"Close now to the armory, very close," Oin muttered to himself as he led the captives deeper and deeper into the tunnel network.

Zarn sniffed the air, then lifted his hand in signal to Chausseur. Chausseur grabbed Manaloul's shoulder from behind and pulled him into the cover of an outcropping of granite. Oin looked back to see if his companions still followed, then he came to an abrupt halt. Two large Night Stalkers stopped the skinny Sea Dweller. They approached from an upper level of the tunnel ahead, and squeezed their girth into the lower corridor. They stopped to examine the nervous prison guard.

"I smell the flesh of outsiders in this hall," one told him. "My stomach tires of stale bread and dried root."

The other looked around.

"I was just down in the sub levels checking on the prisoners," Oin said quietly. "I must certainly reek of their flesh."

"I would devour you, scales and all, just to taste the oils of outsider flesh, if it weren't for *her* orders," the other said, to which Oin could only continue smiling without making eye contact.

After several moments of unbearable tension the Night Stalkers turned from Oin and climbed back into the opening at the end of the tunnel. Dust and small rock fragments broke free from the dripping ceiling and crumbled to the ground with as the Stalkers lumbered on the above level. Oin dashed to the prisoners' hiding place.

"That was too close," he said, out of breath. "The path to the armory will be filled with many hungry Night Stalkers."

Manaloul looked on disapprovingly.

"Is there no other way to the upper levels than through these tunnels?"

Oin thought about the question with mock deliberation.

"There is another path," he said reluctantly, "through the core. It is very dangerous and very hot."

"Let's take the path through the mountain's core then," Chausseur said as he rose. "We are unarmed and unable to defend against the Night Stalkers."

"*And* they most certainly *wouldn't* show mercy to a slave traitor either," Manaloul added.

Oin closed his fish-like eyes, then opened them again after a moment of consideration.

"You're right," he said. "They are heartless, merciless brutes. We will make way to the mountain's core. However, you must follow my every move. There are few who know the path. It is so dangerous the Night Stalkers don't use it."

CHAPTER SEVENTEEN
Surprise Attack

Tucker stood on a rocky ledge high above a raging battle. The sky was scorched and rippled with flaming arrows and blasts of energy. Night Stalkers dove in even rows of flight, bombarding the tiny soldiers below with waves of Red Crystal fire. Swords clashed and spears flew. The air was alive with the smell of blood and the screams of terror. He had a wand in his hand, only it didn't feel like *his* wand. It was unfamiliar to his touch, glowing so brightly that its sheen would not allow Tucker to glimpse into the true color of the crystal essence behind it. He knew in his heart that this wand could end the war, yet he was reluctant to use it. He held the wand at arm's length and closed his eyes.

There was a moment of blackened silence, and then the setting changed around him. Tucker recognized the place immediately. It was the Hidden Village of the Forest Farrows. The mind-tingling reality that he was dreaming overtook him as he scanned his surroundings. Manaloul was there as was Chausseur. Treol, Vanle, Throul, and Shreif were busy in preparation. The looming presence of war hung heavily in the still, breeze-less air. Although no words were spoken, Tucker knew this was to be his next destination. Then he took a step backward and lost his footing. He found himself tumbling blindly off a startlingly high cliff.

Tucker woke to the sickening sensation of actually falling. His limp body was violently shaken by the Adacore's sudden change in direction. He gripped the creature's neck in confusion, haunted by the vision of his dream. His eyes quickly adjusted to the dark skies around them, and the mind numbing recollection of being close to the Nocoule mainland. They touched down onto the black water surface with a splash. Treol was also awakened by the disturbance, and he popped his head out of Tucker's pocket to assess the situation.

"Are we under attack?" he asked.

Tucker remained silent even though the feeling in his consciousness confirmed that they were indeed being hunted. He looked behind as four menacing shadows dipped below the crimson Nocoule horizon.

"We've got at least four," Tucker whispered.

Treol scrambled to ready his bow.

"I've got a few black-tipped arrows," he said, "made them while we were recovering at the Port of Thieves. They should work their way deep into the fur of our enemy, then explode with Silver Crystal energy once inside."

"This darkness is going to work against us Treol. Be sharp."

Tucker turned the floating Adacore around to face the oncoming attack. Then he pulled his cloak hood up over his face.

"Be steady," he whispered. "Fire on my cue. I can feel them around us."

Treol steadied his bow and slowly pulled a black tipped arrow back with the string.

"I'm ready on your mark," he whispered.

"Hold," Tucker replied, "hold steady."

Tucker continued his tense inactivity until the feeling of the repulsive beasts dominated his senses. He could almost taste their awful filth, even though his eyes gave no indication of imminent approach. They closed in, sailing silently in from above them.

"Now!" Tucker shouted as he held up his shimmering white wand.

Treol's black tipped arrow ripped through the silence and arrived deep into its target's flesh just as Tucker unleashed a powerful blast of wind and water skyward. The Night Stalkers were caught off guard. The two on the outermost flank broke off and Tucker saw their shimmering red wands. The center Stalker, presumably their chieftain, was caught by the explosion of water. The black tipped arrow sent the lifeless body into the sea with a loud

Night Of The Stalkers

splash concurrent with the dissipation of the wall of water. Treol reloaded and sent another arrow sailing upward, and it parted the remaining Night Stalkers as the arrow sailed safely between them. Tucker sent up another flurry of wind driven water; however, the Night Stalkers regrouped beneath the spread of the spell's effect. Sizzling balls of flame and smoke came raining down on them; many smoldered with a loud hisses as they hit the cool water.

Tucker sent the Adacore racing skyward, and its massive wings pulled them further from the water's surface with each exaggerated flap. The Night Stalkers changed direction just as quickly and formed a tight grouping behind and slightly below the Adacore's tail. Tucker turned to send a blast of wind into their open wings as Treol released another arrow. This time it found its target, sinking into the closest Stalker's neck just below the back of its head. The creature shrieked and scrambled to remove the dart with its free hand when a tiny flash of silver light escaped its black fur coat. Stunned or destroyed, the creature's body flailed limply in the wind gust Tucker had summoned.

"That's it, Treol!" he said excitedly. "That's team work!"

The last two Stalkers charged them harder. They fired several blasts of hot energy as they approached. Tucker commanded the Adacore to begin a steep banked dive. Speed mounted throughout the descent. Tucker closed his eyes and held onto the Adacore's neck with all of his strength. The giant bird sliced across the water's surface. Its lower wing cut a long arc of white foam as it flew over the water. Just as Tucker was about to come around to face his attackers, a something exploded into his consciousness. Something savage and primal was clearly disturbed by all of the commotion. Instinctively, he sent the Adacore skyward. He passed in front of the Night Stalkers without unleashing an offensive attack. Something was coming. It was coming now. He saw it in his mind. He looked behind the wing of the Adacore. The water broke and there was an explosion of white water closely followed by rows of razor sharp teeth. The mouth continued climbing skyward. From the corner of his eye, he saw a column of shiny black skin.

"A giant sea snake!" Treol cried out.

The Night Stalkers turned at once. Their wide leathery wings opened to full capacity. One vanished into the snake's clamping jaws just before the giant serpent toppled into the water. The splash made a deafening noise. Tucker continued to send the Adacore skyward until thick gray storm clouds surrounded them. Although blind from the heavy fog, they continued upward until the mist weakened. After they broke through the cloud cover into a beautifully starry night, Tucker leveled flight of the Adacore. His heart was pounding, and he let out a long sigh of relief. A black canvass of millions of twinkling lights surrounded them and reached out to meet the glowing horizon. They survived the night and were safely above the storm clouds at dawn's first light.

Night Of The Stalkers

Oin removed small pile of rocks away from a domed dead-end at one of the many identical tunnels through which they had been traveling. Each stone he removed showed more of what was beyond, as the bright orange glow on the other side of the barrier grew stronger. In addition to the light, waves of intense heat poured into the damp cave.

"The core of the mountain is very steep. Don't look down. Follow me closely. This shaft leads in many different directions."

As the final few stones were thrown aside, Oin found an opening not much larger than he was that gatewayed a world of rippling hot gasses and blinding orange light. The wiry Sea Dweller entered first and quickly disappeared from view. Chausseur and Zarn followed and forced themselves through the tiny bright port. Manaloul went last, his large flat gray feet slipped on the tiny stone ledge beyond. He used his cloak to shield his face from the plume of hot gases that rose from the swirling pool of lava beneath them. The ledge on which they stood on was no wider than a foot. It appeared to spiral upward along the smooth walls of the shaft until it gave way to a tiny circle of morning lit sky shining above them.

"We're in the center of the volcano," Manaloul grumbled.

Oin limberly shuffled along the weak ledge leaving the rest of the party to time their steps carefully. One misstep was all it would take to tumble to doom. The rising gasses made it difficult for them to breathe, and also made it harder to spot the next step along the crumbling edge. While he was not quite as carefree as Oin, Chausseur's light steps, balance, and grace sharply contrasted Zarn's gait. Zarn shuffled sideways with his back pressed firmly against the smooth stone walls. The quartet inched their way around the vast open shaft, one cautious footstep at a time, until they finally came to a spot where Oin knelt to feel the stone wall with the palms of his hands.

"Here," he said. "This should be the back wall of the armory."

He carefully dug his scaly fingers into the loose stone and began to clear another opening. The port was cool and shadowy against the red hot air around them. It was difficult for *any of them* to imagine a more awful place in all of Zooblatia, although rumors of the forsaken land *beyond* the volcano's walls made them wonder. Oin slipped carelessly into the dark opening, followed by the others. By the time Manaloul entered, Chausseur had already recovered his long sword and shield from the dozen or so racks. The room was cool and dank, filled to the brink with various weapons of all races and craft. Some Manaloul recognized immediately. Others looked odd and useless. There were wooden clubs with leather grips and heavy chain laden sickles. Wooden shelves housed swords of many lengths and descriptions. Along side, these hung rows of highly decorated bows.

"Take any weapons you can carry," Manaloul directed. "Remember, it will be a perilous journey out of these halls."

Zarn collected various pieces of armor, many of which appeared heavier and shinier than the equipment he had worn into the battle. He picked up a heavy iron mace and took several practice swings with it before he attached it to his hip. Oin chose a long twisted dagger and slipped a suit of chain mail over his scaly teal skin. Chausseur took only the weapons and armor taken from him.

"These are family heirlooms," he said as he realized Manaloul was watching him. "If the Night Stalkers want to lay claim to them, they will have to pry them from my lifeless body."

Zarn snorted excitedly from an isle several shelves from where Manaloul stood.

"Manaloul!" he called out in a raspy voice. "Come have a look at this."

Manaloul approached the shelf with deep interest. Amidst a tangle of arrows, broken spear shafts, and spades, was the unmistakable shape of a crystal wand. Manaloul picked it up and examined the object carefully. It felt cold and light to his touch. A layer of dust had settled upon it. He rolled the solid black tube between his thumb and forefinger and concentrated on all the crystal combinations of which he was aware. After several moments, he opened his eyes to discover the wand remained cold and colorless.

"I fear whatever crystal essence was in this wand has been extinguished," he said.

He slipped the wand into his robes and returned to Chausseur who had just finished gearing-up with weapons and armor.

CHAPTER EIGHTEEN
Twilight Bay

    Tucker and Treol had a breakfast of meat and root with a refreshing drink of cordial while the dual sun's warmth burned away the night's chill from their backs. The storm clouds began to thin as they became more distanced from Nocoule. By midmorning, they had a perfect view of the blue water far below them. The Adacore drifted along the warm tropical breeze that brought them a breath of fresh morning air. Tucker was feeling increasingly calm and confident with his decision to travel in this direction. In fact, the serenity in the air reminded him of the same emotion that surged through his visions. There was no doubt in his mind that this was where his instincts wear leading him. A small island of dense green forest and steep rocky walls appeared in the distance. The Adacore responded immediately and gradually lowered altitude. The horror of Nocoule faded to the recesses of Tucker's mind as excitement of the new island began to build. Tucker wished he could have further explored his vision so he would know the person to seek once he arrived. The Adacore landed softly on a tall rocky outcropping just off the island's noisy shore. It was a short hike down to a valley clearing below where he found a busy village.

He entered the village from the wilderness as a cloaked and hooded stranger, weaving his way between the clusters of stout log homes with wide sweeping tiled roofs. All around the homes were overgrown juts of dense tropical forest. The air was sweet with fruit and honey, occasionally stirred by a warm sea breeze shaking palm leaves in its wake. The hard working residents did not notice the stranger passing along the lane. Some of them busily tended to gardens, while others rolled big sheets of tan dough on tree stumps. They looked almost like Sea Dwellers to Tucker's eyes, except their scales were shades of red and brown instead of green. Their heads, forearms and ankles were outlined with tiny spikes. Tucker sensed their peaceful and honest nature. They weren't just tolerant of his uninvited arrival, they accepted it. He walked aimlessly for nearly an hour observing the incredible people. Then he came to a lane leading to a small grassy hut on the outskirts of the village. He felt excited as he approached the hut. He was certain this was the spot he was instructed to reach through his visions.

"Treol!" he exclaimed. "I believe this is our stop! Stay hidden, but be ready for anything."

As he approached the hut, the front entrance flap quickly lifted. A smooth gray arm signaled him to enter. Tucker bent at the waist and entered the shady dome trying to see the stranger who welcomed him. His mind raced with confusion and his heart began to pound as he laid eyes upon the creature. Its four orb-like eyes, elephant-like skin, and curved head registered immediately. *It looked just like Manaloul!*

"Welcome," the creature said softly. "I've been expecting you."

Tucker was too emotionally startled to reply.

"You are shyer than I expected. May I be so bold as to ask a stranger what troubles him?"

"You look exactly like someone I know," Tucker explained. "He's a good friend of mine. Perhaps you've heard of him. His name is Manaloul."

"Of course I look like him," the smiling stranger said. "He's my father."

Back at the escape, Manaloul heard approaching footsteps and signaled to Chausseur who grinned with delight at possible confrontation. The Battle Cat drew its sword slowly, savoring each passing second. The heavy wooden door to the armory was flung open. An unsuspecting Night Stalker stepped through the frame directly into the path of Chausseur's airborne sword. It pierced the creature's throat before it had an opportunity to groan. Chausseur removed his sword from the throat of the creature and left the stiff lifeless body to fall over forward. It crashed nosily on the stone floor at his feet.

"I can only hope," he said as he wiped his sword clean with the back of his paw, "that the mercy I have shown you with a quick death was extended to my cousin."

At the hut on the island, Tucker extended his hand and accepted the cup of steaming herbal tea. His mind churned with surprise.

"Manaloul never spoke of offspring," he said as he blew the spiral of steam from the top of the cup.

"I suspect he would not. My name is Dominus. My father believes I perished in a Wyvern ambush."

"Surely, the Green Crystal *must* have made him aware you still live," Tucker interrupted.

"His devotion to the vision of the Green Crystal is so great, he is blind to much of the world around him. If he would focus his thoughts on locating me, the crystal would reveal to him that I live. Nevertheless, alas, I wish not for such things to unfold. I shamed him in life by my actions, and he deserves the peace of believing I am gone."

Tucker drew a deep breath and forced himself to take a long sip of his tea. His mind raced with questions he would refrain from asking. If Dominus was anything like Manaloul, the answers would come over time.

"Do you not wonder who I am?

"Are you not the successor to King Harvey's throne?" Dominus asked.

"I am," Tucker said.

"I apologize for my casual demeanor," Dominus replied. "This prophecy was told me long ago in my travels. Once I *also* shared in my father's devotion to the Green Crystal. In fact, I was inducted into the Order of the Crystalline for my work. I was a scribe, young king. My role was to document all that was known about the crystals and their effects. I was one of many who devoted their lives to the study of a science beyond explanation. We did not attempt reason that which was unreasonable, nor did we try to explain that which was beyond explanation."

Tucker struggled to remember Manaloul's dissertation on the Order of the Crystalline in his head.

"We were witnesses to the phenomenon," Dominus continued, "nothing more. I regret to say I became involved with a new study that came about as we began to understand what made the crystals react."

"Alchemy," Tucker interrupted.

Dominus froze in surprise.

"Indeed!" he shouted. "You know our history as a true king should. Alchemy, ah yes, that blasted concept would save my life, and disgrace my family name. You see, I was banned from the

Order just before they were ambushed and killed. Part of my secret punishment was that I was marooned on this remote island, so my research could not be continued. The Order was afraid of what I discovered. They were afraid that if crystals could be manufactured synthetically, they could be wrongfully exploited. The knowledge could fall into the wrong hands. They believed the crystals could be used to control. The populace could be controlled through fear of the unknown."

"This doesn't seem like too bad a place to be marooned," Tucker said and changed the subject.

"It isn't. Many would consider Twilight Bay paradise. Long ago, it was inhabited by Sea Dwellers who made it their rightful home. It was so long ago that their bodies adapted over time. They no longer return to the sea like their distant cousins. They live their entire lives on land. They are a hard-working, honest lot. They care little of the ways of the modern world, and they accepted me with open arms. My life is very different from the life I once had. Sometimes I miss my research; however, I have been content for the most part."

"Then was it *your* research that created the. . ."

"Gold Crystal?" Dominus filled in the words to the question. "Oh yes! My studies were beyond the scope of anything that preceded them, I'm afraid. The Order practically dared me to construct a synthetic crystal, because they were confident it could not be done. They felt failure would discourage me from pursuing the matter. Perhaps I should have listened to them and continued to be satisfied with documenting what I knew *instead* of disturbing it."

He drew a deep breath followed by a long sigh.

"I spent years on the tedious process of aligning element groups until at long last I managed to complete the task. The common elements around us hold the key to channeling energy just like the crystals do, *if* they can arranged correctly. The crystals are neutral in the struggle of good verses evil. It is the will of the beholder that changes their properties. The right combination of simple elements, if focused on wholeheartedly, becomes a catalyst to the flow of energy. This is true everywhere throughout time. The real magic exists within each of us, and it flows through us with each choice we make, and with each silent thought *we* believe is undetectable. My work proved how far the act of focus could be taken to influence crude matter. The Gold Crystal was supposed to f a great scientific accomplishment. However, the Order became uneasy when they discovered one of the Gold Crystal side effects was an explosive release when exposed to one of the oldest known crystals, the Red Crystal."

"I have seen that effect, first hand," Tucker said.

"That side effect is what ultimately put an end to my research. It also stopped any further research on production of synthetic crystals. This was coupled with the realization that the

Night Of The Stalkers

Magenta Crystal carried a deadly side effect to all who encountered it. The senate decided the Gold Crystal was to be taken to the caves of Appelia and cast through a gate it would create. It was forever banished from Zooblatia, and I was stripped of everything I held dear to me, my family, and my wand."

"Dominus, the Gold Crystal has returned."

The humble creature's glassy-eyes widened in surprise as he lowered his cup of steaming tea.

"You know this to be true, young king?"

"Manaloul, your father, insists on this. He has felt its presence."

"In the wrong hands, the Gold Crystal could be extremely dangerous. The senate must be made aware of the threat immediately so they can pass a law to…"

"The senate is no more," Tucker interrupted. "It has been destroyed by unknown assassins."

Dominus slowly sipped his tea. A look of hopelessness crossed his wrinkled face.

"The walls of Losparia have fallen. I come to you today as a refugee to seek your council on what I should do next."

"I am afraid there is little I can say that would be of much use to you. My time with the Gold Crystal was very short. There is little that even I, its creator, understand about its true abilities. However, as long as I live, the power of the Gold Crystal lives, for I alone give it life. This is something no one knows or ever knew, not even my father. Only I know this, and now you know it as well."

Tucker felt his heart sink, and the magnitude of what Dominus was telling him became clear.

"I am hoping you will accompany me back to the Zooblatian mainland. The hour is at hand where the entire world will be thrust into battle. This I have foreseen."

"You must understand, young king; the fate of Zooblatia is no longer my burden to bear. I have been forced to walk away from that role long ago."

"But you said the fate of the Order of the Crystalline would have been your doom had you not been banned. It was they who made the fatal mistake of banishing your work. Your crystal could have ended this conflict long ago."

"My father will never accept me. I am a convicted traitor. You must understand this. I tried to disprove the very thing to which he devoted his entire existence."

"You can't turn your back on Zooblatia in its hour of need. Your father, and all that is good and pure in this world need you, Dominus."

"I am afraid of what my father will say when he learns I live."

"Listen to me, I know your father. He will be overwhelmed with joy to see you again. I miss my family more than anything in

Night Of The Stalkers

the world, even though I doubt I will *ever* have the chance to see them again. Moreover, *they* had only a *fraction* of the love to share with me, their only son, that Manaloul has for you. My family barely acknowledged me until they learned my destiny in Zooblatia. It was only then they began to respect me, a king. I was no longer *just* some lonely child. And even though they hardly noticed me when I was with them, I would give *anything* to see them again."

Dominus sat silent for a long moment of internal conflict.

"You say the Gold Crystal returned to this land. I have one question that drives my heart to aiding you, young king. Who in Zooblatia wields my Gold Crystal?"

"That I don't know," Tucker said. "But I assure you that we intend to find out."

CHAPTER NINETEEN

Into the Night

Chausseur and Zarn barred the heavy door shut with a spear they chose from one of the weapon racks. Even with their combined weights pressed firmly against the doors, the doors shook in rhythm and spilt clouds of rolling dust from their cracks.

"I don't know how much longer this door will hold," Manaloul said as he looked at the others who continued to bombard the door. "I sense many of our enemy outside, and there are more gathering behind those."

Manaloul calmly meditated in the middle of the crowded room. His wand glowed brightly. It emitted an eerie green light that washed over the room and made the shadows of the weapons racks grow long against the stone walls. At once, he opened his eyes and stood to his feet.

"Move away from the door," he announced.

Chausseur glanced skeptically at Zarn. Then the pair stepped away from the door in unison. With a metallic drag, Chausseur

Night Of The Stalkers

unsheathed his sword. He swung it precisely through the stale air. The doors heaved from the sudden force applied from beyond it, but they held shut. Zarn gripped his heavy mace with both hands. He cracked his knuckles as he released and re-gripped the handle in secession. The heavy wooden doors again bowed inward. This time the spear that was wedged across the doors snapped in an explosion of splintered wood. The doors swung violently open. A sea of black matted fur poured into the opening like water through a floodgate.

Chausseur calmly swung his broad sword. He connected with several of his targets in a stunning display of finesse and precision. In contrast, Zarn swung wildly a few feet from Chausseur, his mace occasionally missed its target and stuck soundly into the wooden door. Manaloul unleashed a sparkling wave of green energy that glanced into the leading row of Night Stalkers who were in the process of stepping over their fallen kindred. Their eyes faded into blank lifeless stares as they toppled over and fell into the pile of furry corpses.

"Now!" Manaloul shouted to Oin who kicked away the few remaining stones that partially obstructed the escape hatch leading into the mountain's fiery shaft.

Despite the increasingly large pile of slain Night Stalkers, the flow of inwardly pushing bodies kept coming. The stone frame around the wooden doors started to crumble. At least ten of them were inside the room forcing streams of hot flame from the tips of their twisted wands. Shelves exploded on contact, sending red-hot weapons spinning wildly about the room. Chausseur blocked an expanding ring of fire with his shield, then returned a death blow by throwing his sword directly between a Night Stalker's beady eyes. As he retrieved his weapon a dozen more Stalkers forced their way inside.

"Make for the shaft!" Manaloul hollered amidst the commotion.

Oin went through as did Manaloul. Chausseur signaled for Zarn to go next. Then he turned to face the soldiers. He raised his broad shield. Flames and smoke engulfed the front of his shield, making the inside of it hot to the touch. He waited until Zarn slipped through the opening, then he went in backwards. As he stepped through, something solid bounced off his shield. The group found themselves again on the terribly narrow ledge high above the pool of bubbling lava. The heat instantly took their breath away, and the burning in their eyes caused them to seek protection for them. They covered their eyes with their wrists.

"Oin," Manaloul commanded, "lead us up to the mouth of this volcano."

The frightened guard reluctantly inched forward.

"They'll follow us here," he said. "What chance do we have on this narrow ledge with our backs against the wall?"

Night Of The Stalkers

"They do not use these paths. Our passing will be safe."

Chausseur turned back just as the narrow entrance exploded outward. There was a great a cloud of dust. Chunks of gray stone tumbled freely into the red abyss. Night Stalkers began squeezing into the shaft. Each spread its massive wings and flew as it stepped off the twisty edge.

"They've come through!" Chausseur yelled frantically.

"Hold your ground!" Manaloul demanded. "Just keep your faces shielded from the intense heat."

"But," Oin began to protest just as the first Night Stalker through caught a blast of heat plume across its widely spread wings.

The creature spun wildly upward before smashing soundly against the smooth rock wall on the far side of the shaft. Then it tumbled limply alongside its wand and vanished, as it fell down into the thick smoke. The second Night Stalker tucked its head and flapped its wings harder. It rocketed past them and continued climbing in effort to break free of the volcano's mouth. It tried not to suffer the same fate as the first monstrous bird. It made it just shy of the evening sky, and then its wings inflated with a blast of hot gas and it was impaled on a jagged spike hanging from the domed opening. A third tried to escape the fates of the first two. It scurried back into the tiny opening after *it* witnessed the shaft's effect on its partners, and it clung helplessly by its finger tips to the edge of the crude opening as its legs flailed in panic. It screamed in terror, but no assistance from the pack standing just beyond it in the armory came. Oin marched them onward. The squealing of the falling creature echoed from the walls.

"They'll work their way through the corridors inside and try to intercept us at the top. We must make haste."

Chausseur hopped along while pieces of the ledge broke and crumbled beneath his feet. It was a slow winding climb to the top. After three full revolutions around the perimeter of the cavern, they made it. Hot air rushed in wild turbulence as it funneled through the opening into the gray skies. Oin gripped the rocky lip of the opening in an effort to pull himself free. The updraft caught him, and he flew out of the opening. He landed on his back on the steep rocky hillside outside and slid with a pile of rolling rock and ash several feet down the side of the volcano. He turned back to witness Manaloul's rupture from the crater. He landed on his back as well and slid down the rocky embankment. Zarn launched free from the opening and landed soundly on his shoulder. He somersaulted several times and stopped next to Manaloul. Only Chausseur landed gracefully on his feet.

"We're out," he said as he looked back at the steady stream of erupting gas and smoke. "Where do we go now."

"Who would think to find us here?" Zarn snorted.

Night Of The Stalkers

"We are being sought out even as we speak;" Manaloul answered them calmly, "a small band of rescuers needs only a sign to hone in on us."

"A sign?" Oin asked. "What sign can we send from up here?"

Manaloul stood calmly. He brushed his robes and sent clouds of brown dust rolling away from him.

"Leave that to me," he said.

He made his way back up the steep slope of crumbling shale and stopped halfway between the ledge and the wide mouth of the volcano. He took out his wand and closed his eyes, and sent it into an immediate green shimmer. After a few moments of silent meditation, he released a wobbling ball of green light that moved slowly skyward. It arced forward as it ascended then it dropped from sight into the smoking gap. Manaloul casually returned to the ledge and told everyone to shield their eyes. The volcano erupted in a flash of blinding white light that bleached Chausseur's vision even through the cover of his inner elbow. The light then focused itself into a streaming column of bright green smoke that poured itself upon the clouds high in the above sky. For an instant, the entire land was illuminated. It was a disturbingly empty endless plain of craggy rock formations and smoking volcanoes. Oin shivered at the lifeless vision of Nocoule.

"What do you suppose that is?" Dominus asked from his position behind Tucker on the Adacore.

Tucker turned and saw the string of green light high in the red and black clouds of Nocoule far off to their north.

"That, my friend, is hope," Tucker replied as he squinted through the misting rains.

Manaloul waved emphatically in the direction of an aerial rescue brigade that appeared over the ridge in response to his signal. A small fleet of speedy sparrows with Forest Farrows mounted on their backs broke the ridge and darted downward. Behind them the unmistakable flapping of Adacore wings came, led by the erratic fluttering of a thoroughly exhausted Petri.

"Our rescue party arrives!" Manaloul exclaimed with relief. "We've been on this wasteland just about long enough!"

CHAPTER TWENTY

The Gathering

Tucker arrived at the shore of Zooblatia about a half a day behind Manaloul and company. His old friend starred in awe as his Adacore roughly set down. Its powerful legs came to a standstill in the warm sand.

"Father it's me," Dominus announced timidly.

"Son," Manaloul said in reply, his usual tone of confidence was cracked and broken.

"I was marooned by the Order of the Crystalline before they were destroyed long ago. It was I who created the Golden Crystal, father. I was lost from civilization until our king found and rescued me."

"I know," Manaloul said. "Somehow I've always known you escaped the Wyvern attack. I dared not use the Green Crystal to confirm word of your death, for if it did there would have been little hope left in the world for this old wizard. As long as I had the hope you were somewhere out there, I had the strength to continue."

Night Of The Stalkers

Dominus slid off the Adacore's back and ran into his father's embrace.

"I dreamt of this day," Manaloul said. "My deepest hope is now a reality!"

Petri suddenly emerged from among the group and hastily perched himself on Tucker's shoulder.

"Your majesty!" he cried out. "I just knew I would see you again!"

"If what they tell me is true, then I have a lot to thank you for, old buddy," Tucker replied as he stroked the bird's smooth green feathers. "You've made me proud."

Tucker dismounted his Adacore in the still serenity of the Hidden Village and took a deep breath of the clean fresh air. The village was alive with the celebration of their safe return. The early morning sky erupted with a display of raining silver shower. Fires crackled noisily. Their smoke slowly moved across the streams of light that filtered through the trees. Treol scampered off to his excited kin and left Tucker a moment of solitude on the sandy shore of the quiet bay. He felt a tear of relief roll down his cheek as the events that led him here faded into his memory, not unlike a twisted nightmare from which it was a relief to have escaped. The land was calm. There was a stillness Tucker could only liken to the calm before a storm. In the distance a rumble of thunder sounded. They were out there regrouping for their final assault on Zooblatia.

Night Of The Stalkers

A tiny Farrow villager sprinted to the side of Tucker.

"Your majesty," he said, "Shreif and Manaloul seek your presence in council. Shall I tell them you will answer?"

"Yes, of course," Tucker said. "Tell them I'll be right there."

"Very good your majesty," the Farrow said.

Tucker took a final moment to stare across the open sea and to allow his weary body to glory in the feeling that he was back where he belonged. The task of war was again at hand. Now, they only hoped to have some time.

Tucker entered the heart of the village and found a large gathering of familiar faces. Several Zoobles sat in a loose circle beside two highly decorated Sea Dweller representatives. Dozens of Grainda troops were scattered about the camp, as was a spider merchant, much smaller than Lucinda, who nervously spun a tight ball of web with her front legs. Chausseur sat next to Manaloul and Oin joined the gathering.

"Free people of Zooblatia," Shreif proudly announced, "it is with great pleasure that I give to you your king!"

The air filled with cheer, and the crowd bowed in unison.

"Please!" Tucker cried out in embarrassment. "Arise, my friends. I approach not as your king, but as an ally to a common enemy."

Manaloul approved and said, "The time has come where we as free races of this land will unite in battle. You have been summoned to represent your people under one king, and to make them proud."

Tucker absorbed the powerful words of Manaloul.

"Time is already against us, and while we are all grateful to be here unharmed, our initial raid on the Nocoule mainland was not a victory. There is a new threat to democracy rising across the sea. They have struck the first blow, and a mighty blow it was. The Halls of Losparia stand no longer."

There were many gasps around the group and whispered chatter.

"But our enemy underestimated the cunning of our king," he continued, to which the crowd again began to cheer. "Today we must begin the task of preparing a battle plan. Our enemy is ruthless, cunning, and powerful. Only by uniting as free people do we stand a chance against them."

"Chausseur," Shreif interrupted, "you are to be named general of the free army of Zooblatia."

The Battle Cat bowed in respect. His tail danced vigorously.

"Treol," the Farrow continued, "you are given the honor of First Guard and loyal defender of our king. You have shown valor that is unrivaled among your people."

Tucker smiled at his loyal companion.

"And Petri, royal assistant to his majesty, you have become an honorary scout bringing word of this news to our secluded ears."

Night Of The Stalkers

The crowd stood in applause, and Tucker felt a rush of excitement surge through him. The doubts of his influence over the kingdom faded to the moment of their cheer. There was again a purpose to the cruel tasks at hand and assurance that not all was dark and hopeless.

"Son," Manaloul said softly to Dominus, "I believe you'll need this."

He handed him the wand he collected in the armory. It sparkled to green life in Dominus' hand.

"But I thought. . ."

"No thoughts on the matter. You will need it if you are to continue your research."

"I have turned from that path, father."

"No! You were forced from it by those who were closed minded. It is clear to me the fruits of your labor not only saved your life, but brought two worthy kings to Zooblatia when they were needed most. Resuming your research will most certainly prove essential in the restoration of peace to these lands."

Shreif stood again with Vanle and Throul by his side and said, "Stone walls can be rebuilt, and new governments can be formed. On this day we have many thanks to give. On this eve of the greatest battle of our time let us celebrate our freedom as a reminder of that for which we will all be fighting."

Night Of The Stalkers

www.ingramcontent.com/pod-product-compliance
Ingram Content Group UK Ltd.
Pitfield, Milton Keynes, MK11 3LW, UK
UKHW041953230426
12048UKWH00008B/310